WHITE
NOISE

WHITE NOISE

TANYA LISLE

SCRAP PAPER ENTERTAINMENT

CHAPTER ONE

IT WAS JUST an off morning. His phone had shut off all alarms for the day, he fell out of bed when his mom came to wake him up, and he burnt his hand on the toaster, but that was all over now. He'd leave his house and have to concentrate on school and friends soon enough. Everything would be normal soon.

There was definitely no one out there looking for him, no matter how much he felt like there was.

Max fumbled with the laces on his shoes. He couldn't just slide them on today, instead having to untie the laces and sit there to tie them back up. At least he wasn't late yet.

"Are you home tonight?" his mother asked him. "Your father's home early and he said he wanted to try something different for dinner." She sat next to him, pulling on her own shoes for work and putting a pair of heels in her bag. Max looked at her, his mom looking back, her red hair pulled into a strict bun and the smile on her freckled face not quite meeting her eyes.

Though he looked more like his father, Max had his mother's colouring and shared most of her expressions. He knew the one she wore now well.

"I don't have to be," Max said. He finally got his laces back in order and picked up his backpack. "Especially if it's anything like the tuna casserole."

"To be fair, the recipe did not specify *canned* tuna."

"I'll just go to Jeremy's house tonight."

"If you don't have training tonight, you're coming home. You aren't going to let your mother be the only one with food poisoning, are you?"

"You aren't going to let your only son get food poisoning again, are you?"

"If you don't have lifeguarding tonight, then you're coming home," she said. "Who knows? It might be good."

"So pizza if it goes wrong?"

"Pizza," she agreed. She let Max out the door first, locking it behind both of them.

While she drove off, Max made his way down the street, trying to figure out why his feet felt funny. That nagging feeling that something was wrong today wouldn't leave him, so he did his best to ignore it.

He went to Tara's house and knocked. "Hey," she said after yelling her goodbyes into the house. "You look awful..." She was out a moment later, looking him over and tilting her head at his shoes.

Max followed her eyes down and saw what had her confused. Of course his shoes were on the wrong feet. He sat down on the front step of her house and switched them. "It's been a bad morning."

"What did you do to him?"

Max looked up as he finished his laces and saw Jeremy coming over from a few doors down. He had his backpack slung over one shoulder and looked at Tara with a grin creeping across his face under his crooked nose. He was limping a bit from a fall in a basketball game a week before, but still pounded a fist into his hand like he was planning to make Tara pay.

"He did it to himself," Tara said, smiling.

Sometimes he wondered why the two of them didn't just date already.

Max got to his feet and started walking to school, the other two falling in step beside him. He felt better with the two of them with him, if only because someone would be able to stop him from doing any other incredibly stupid things this morning.

The smile had not left Tara's face. "So besides forgetting how shoes work..."

"Had a run in with the floor and a toaster this morning, too,"

Max said, holding up his hand to show them the burn. When he looked, it had already faded away. "Something's just off today."

"Forget your meds?" Jeremy offered.

And then he realized. His alarms didn't go off. He'd forgotten to take his Adderall.

Today was going to suck.

He glanced back at his house, but he wasn't going to head back now. He could handle one day without it. Instead, he took out his phone and set an alarm to remember to take it when he got home.

"Even if he did forget, he's never this off," Tara said.

"Maybe he's going to discover he's Batman today."

"You mean my parents are going to get shot?" Max asked, pocketing his phone. Jeremy didn't hear him.

"Except you're not cool enough for Batman. Maybe Robin."

"So who's Batman?" Tara asked.

"Me, obviously. You can be Batgirl. You'd look better in the costume."

"I really need more girl friends."

"Yeah, but they wouldn't be as much fun as us," Max said. He let his mind wander into the conversation and away from whatever was wrong with him this morning. That feeling that someone was looking for him still lingered in his mind, but discussions about superheroes were enough of a distraction to keep him from obsessing over it.

The feeling of someone looking for him didn't return until they got to school. Outside the door he spotted a woman dressed in an all white pantsuit and her black hair pulled back. She conferred with two others, these all dressed in black and moving their hands rapidly at one another. None of their mouths were moving.

"Deaf goths?" Tara asked as they walked past them and into the school. "That's new."

"You think they're new?" Max asked, trying to push back his unease. She might be the one looking for him, but he still didn't know why anyone would be looking for him. As near as he could tell, there was no reason anyone would want him.

Jeremy shrugged. "Maybe? You finish the math homework from last night?"

It's just the lack of meds talking, he told himself. *Except that not taking them doesn't make you paranoid.*

———◆———

OVER THE COURSE of the day, he got used to the feeling of someone trying to find him. He was not difficult to find. If they really wanted to talk to him, all they had to do was go to the office and pretend to be his parents or someone important.

They were in the halls all day, just wandering around the school between classes. The woman in white was only ever with one of them at a time, he noticed, while one of the two kids she watched would be off on his own somewhere else. No one paid attention to them beyond getting a good look at them, the school never having seen anyone in full goth attire before. The chains, spikes and dark hair falling in their eyes on top of an entirely black ensemble was not in fashion right now — especially not in the late May heat.

At lunch, he met up with Tara, Jeremy and the rest of his friends, but could not stop thinking about what the goth kids and the woman in white were really doing here. They barely said anything about them, leaving Max to quietly speculate on it while his friends talked about upcoming finals and plans for the weekend. He could barely bring himself to care about what was happening in his classes today, much less what the week-end held. From what scraps he heard, it sounded like a lot of studying. The girls were going to Ashley's house tonight, since her parents were going to be away, and they were going to make a party out of it with none of the guys.

Maybe the woman in white was like the special needs teacher for the two goth kids. He imagined they needed one who knew sign language. Or maybe she was their social worker, trying to force them to attend classes and failing because one was con-stantly running away. They looked old enough to be seniors, if not older.

It all had nothing to do with him, of course. So why did he still feel like there was someone looking for him?

He spotted another one of them again roaming the halls while he was getting his Chemistry books from his locker and no woman in white in sight. That paranoia of someone looking for him got stronger and Max tried desperately to ignore it.

He turned away and heard a familiar yelp behind him. He turned back and saw Ashley, one of his friends, bump into the goth kid. She fell back and dropped her books, her binder splitting open on impact with the ground.

Max went to help, the goth kid bending down to help get her papers together. It was quick, Max handing her a stack and the goth guy handing her another one, keeping his head bowed. His hands alternated between a closed fist rubbing his chest and pressing both palms together in prayer and bowing.

"It's okay," Ashley said, backing away from him slowly into Max. "I should have been looking."

The goth guy looked up and smiled gently, rubbing his fist on his chest again. Underneath the fringe of hair, red eyes looked back at them.

Ashley jumped back into Max. The goth guy noticed and held his hands up, backing away slowly.

"Let's get to class," Max said, ushering her along and nodding to the goth guy as he turned away. No, if he was looking for Max, he would have done something. Instead, he turned away and went back to his slow meander through the busy halls.

"Did you see his eyes?" Ashley asked once they were up the stairs. She sounded shaken.

"Yeah," Max said. "Those were some weird contacts."

"Hey, are you busy tomorrow?" she asked, not looking at him.

Max thought about it as he held the door open for her and the next three students that walked into the chemistry lab. "I've got training in the morning, but if you need me after that I can do something. What's up?"

"Uh... math!" she said. "I need some help with math."

"Sure," he said. "I'll give you a call, I guess?"

Ashley nodded and took her seat. Max took out his phone and made a note of it before he forgot, taking his own seat by the window. Tara was already sitting, books out and tapping her pen against the textbook as she tried to finish the reading for today. She barely paid attention to him as he set his bag down and took out his own books, their teacher beginning the lesson shortly after.

Max could not bring himself to care about the lesson. There was an experiment to do and while their teacher explained how they were supposed to do it, he kept thinking back to that goth guy. He felt like something should have happened there. Their eyes should have met and he would realize that it was Max he'd been looking for all day. Something should have changed right there, but he'd walked away so easily.

But there was no one looking for him.

"Can you stop with the leg?" Tara asked, glaring at his bouncing leg before looking back at him. "It's really distracting."

"Huh?" Max hadn't even realized he was doing it. How long had he been doing that? "Sorry."

"You were doing it all through lunch, too. Are you okay?"

"Fine. Why?"

"Because now that I know how dangerous that stuff is, I'm not touching it. I'll take notes."

Max pulled on the gloves and looked at the chemicals in front of him. Each was labeled with masking tape and felt pen, and he knew he had to put them together somehow. Somehow. "What am I doing?"

Tara let out a frustrated sigh and slowly walked him through the first step of the experiment, passing him her notes for the procedure so he could follow on his own. Acid and a base to cause a reaction. There was a chance of a severe injury if they did it wrong or spilled it on themselves. Sometimes he wondered why anyone would let teenagers, fire and chemicals interact under such poorly supervised conditions.

"Max? Leg."

"Sorry," he said, forcing his leg still. He continued to try to measure out the liquids, but it was so tedious and he could feel Tara and half the class watching him struggle to get the levels just right. He was pretty good at estimating. He could probably get them about right without staring at the meniscus like a dork.

"So what's the plan for tonight?" Tara asked.

"What?"

"The guys are getting together to do something, right?"

"Oh. Don't know."

He could feel Tara looking at him, but he didn't look back. There was an experiment to do. Things to boil. He needed to concentrate on not blowing this stuff up. He checked the notes for what he needed to add next.

"You are completely out of it today. Seriously, is everything okay?"

"Fine," he said quickly. He let out a breath and poured the chemicals into the larger heated vial. If anyone was going to not call him a dumbass, it was Tara. "You ever feel like you're being watched?"

"That's probably just Ashley," Tara said. "She's been looking over all class."

"I don't think that's it. She just asked me to come by and help her with math tomorrow."

"Oh no, she didn't."

"Didn't what?"

"I'm sorry, but I have to do this now. Max, do you *like* Ashley?"

"What? No! I mean, she's a friend, but not like that. It's just math."

"Why not? She's nice. Cute. Not a total dumbass."

"She's... not my type."

"So what is your type?"

Max frowned and poured the next set of chemicals into the boiling solution. His type? How did this turn into a conversation about his type? He was worried that there were people coming for him even though he couldn't think of any reason behind it. Even now he felt like the woman in white was trying to close in on him with her goth guy henchmen. This was not the time for trying to figure out his love life.

"I don't know why we're talking about this," he said, turning to look at her. "I mean, it's just math. It's not like—"

"Max!" She jumped back, her eyes on the experiment.

Max turned back, already feeling something hot dropping onto his jeans. He pulled his leg back from the steady stream of acid that spilled over from the boiling beaker and tried to push the papers out of the way as it spilled across the desk.

The teacher was by moments later, pulling both of them back from the desk and pushing Max to wash his hands in case he got any acid on them. He cut his pant leg off as well, blisters already forming on his shin. Max rinsed off what he could.

Tara helped him out of class to the nurses office. She carried both of their bags and let Max lean on her, Max limping as the pain settled in. His leg burned, but he gritted his teeth and tried to ignore it as best he could. If someone really was after him right now, he wouldn't be able to fight back. It would be the perfect time for the woman in white to make her move.

Except she isn't looking for me. No one is coming after me.

"Sorry," she said after they were half way down the hall. "But how do you not notice there's acid spilling on your leg?"

"If I remember right, *someone* was distracting me."

"Oh sure, blame me because you were a dumbass."

"No problem."

"What's really going on, Max?" she asked. "This isn't really because Ashley's been staring at you all day. She's done that before. What's really going on?"

"It's just been a really bad day," he told her. "Everyone has them right?"

They said nothing and they kept walking through the halls, getting closer and closer to the nurse's office. Max realized that the paranoia of something coming for him had stopped. Maybe it was because the halls were empty and he couldn't imagine eyes watching him through the crowds. Maybe he finally managed to convince himself that the woman in white wasn't some mysterious figure looking to add him to some secret collection of under aged boys. Whatever it was, he felt the weight lift off of him. Maybe the rest of the day would actually improve.

"Hey, are you sure you need the nurse?" Tara asked. "That looked a lot worse in class."

He looked down at his leg. The blisters were gone, instead leaving a long, very wet scrape. It didn't even hurt that much anymore.

"Just for a band-aid," he said.

Okay, so maybe no one was coming after him, but if they were, this might just be the reason why.

CHAPTER TWO

HIS CELL HAD notoriously bad reception on school grounds. He tried to look up acid burns, but his browser could only tell him how bad the reception was. The phone functions worked, but he wasn't sure how to text Google to find out how worried he should be about spilling acid on his leg.

Unwilling to worry Tara any further, he didn't ask to borrow hers and waited until he was home to look it up. His father's car wasn't in the driveway when he got home so he went straight up to his room, dropping his bag at his bedroom door and looking up the severity of acid burns.

He took off his band-aid to get a better look at it. The scrape had scabbed over and the slight limp he'd walked home with was completely gone.

According to Wikipedia, it was a highly corrosive chemical that should have caused third degree burns on skin contact. He should need a doctor right now. "Don't panic," he told himself, taking a deep breath. "You're just... turning into Wolverine."

The alarm on his phone went off and he took his Adderall before he changed into a pair of shorts. If nothing else, he'd at least be able to concentrate for the evening. That feeling that someone was looking for him was back and he wanted that to go away. He could almost feel the eyes on him from the tree outside his house.

He closed his curtains and kept looking up acid burns for some reason to explain why he got better so quickly. It was definitely blistering when he left class. He didn't want to put any weight on it and every movement sent a shot of pain up his leg. Even the air stung.

When he heard the door open downstairs, he still hadn't found any explanation for it.

"Max?" his dad called from the bottom of the stairs. "You home?"

"Coming!" he called back, locking his computer before heading downstairs. He would figure this out after dinner.

His dad had two large grocery bags on the kitchen counter and started to spread the contents out around the kitchen. He turned back, smiling broadly with a very large piece of something wrapped in brown paper in his hands. Max knew the smell and he was already dreading it.

"Hey, can you help me with dinner?"

"It's not tuna casserole again, is it?" he asked, looking at the wrapped meat.

His dad laughed. "Oh no, not this time. Buddy at work started talking about this great sea bass thing his wife made and it sounded easy enough. I figure there's no harm in giving it a shot. Help me cut up the vegetables."

Max was resigned to his fate — he would help cook the thing that killed him.

He took up a knife and started going to work on the peppers while his dad cleaned the fish in the sink and prepared the dishes. Whenever Max finished with one vegetable, his father would add another to his cutting board. His dad put the news on for some background noise, the report talking about a series of break-ins across the coast occurring in houses where the family was on vacation.

"You'd think they'd take something," his dad commented as the story wrapped up.

"Maybe they're just squatting."

"How was school?"

"Good."

"I got an interesting call from your teacher today," he said.

Max could feel those eyes on him and he tensed up, forcing himself to continue moving the knife. He went over everything he'd done in school that day, trying to figure out what would make them call his father. He didn't cause any trouble as near as he could tell. Didn't skip any classes. There were no tests to have potentially failed.

"Apparently you had a bit of an accident in Chemistry," he continued. "Spilled some acid on your leg. He seemed worried and suggested we might want to take you to the hospital to get it properly checked out."

"Oh. That."

"Since you didn't text, I figured you were fine. Although that does look like a nasty cut."

"It's fine," Max said. "I'm fine."

"Are you still going to be able to go to your lifeguarding tomorrow? Chlorine isn't exactly great for that."

"I'll be fine."

His dad dropped it at that and put the fish in the oven, several vegetables cooking on the stove. "This time," he said. "No getting sick this time. Promise."

Max smiled and nodded before heading back upstairs. He admitted that it looked good this time, but he checked the washroom upstairs just in case to make sure it had an adequate amount of toilet paper and Pepto Bismol.

He went back to his room and opted for homework instead of looking up acid burns even more. Obsessing over it was only going to cut into his time being paranoid about someone watching him from outside his window, not to mention he had Math. He probably had Chemistry, too.

When his parents called him for dinner, he double checked the bathroom before heading downstairs. He thought he saw something move outside the bathroom window and tried to tell himself it was nothing as he headed downstairs to the dinner table.

No one is after you.

His father presented the fish and vegetables to them with a proud smile. Both Max and his mother did their best to look happy about it, but Max could tell she was also thinking about the tuna casserole from last time. This time, at least, everything looked like it had been properly cooked.

"So I got a call from your chemistry teacher today, Max," his mother said as she took a little fish and a large helping of vegetables.

"He's fine," his father said. "There's barely anything there."

His mother took the first bite of the fish and stopped, a look of surprise spreading across her face. "This is actually good."

"You don't think I'd give you food poisoning twice, do you?" his father asked, his smile only growing wider.

Max took that as his cue to try dinner. It was still fish, but it wasn't bad. It was cooked all the way through and it didn't taste too fishy. At the very least, he didn't think he was going to be sick from it. If he wasn't spending his night with his head in the toilet, he was happy.

When he was almost done, his phone buzzed in his pocket. He pulled it out to see the text Jeremy left him. *Raid tonight?*

"Plans?" his father asked.

"Jeremy," he said. "He wants to do a thing. Can I go?"

Both his mother and father dismissed him from the table, Max dumping his dishes in the sink before heading upstairs. Within minutes he had his headphones on with a Dark Elf Rogue on screen running through the town to the guild hall. Jeremy joined him a moment later and they headed out into the woods.

"Hey," Jeremy said, his voice coming through Max's headphones. "So I hear you nearly killed yourself in Chem."

"I just spilled some stuff. It's fine."

"Tara thinks you've been completely out of it all day."

"Tara also thought going out with that guy in a band that one time was a good idea."

"Ouch." He punctuated it by delivering the final blow to an orc and they moved on through the forest. "She's not wrong, though. There's been something with you all day."

Max could almost feel something creeping up on him. The lights were on in his room, but it felt like he was trapped in the dark with a tiger ready to pounce on him. He tried to push the feeling away, but this time it wouldn't go. He looked at the window, finding the curtains shifting softly. Behind them, the window was closed.

"Hey, Max?" Jeremy asked. "You okay over there? I'm getting my ass kicked."

"Oh, right," he said, forcing his attention back to the game. "Sorry."

"Just try to stay focused for five minutes," he said. "What's with you today?"

"Just a weird feeling," he said. "It's like — *Holy sh*—"

He glanced back at his room and saw another guy behind him dressed in black with red eyes. He rammed his chair back into his desk and the guy grabbed him, pulling him away from his computer and his headset falling off. One hand clamped around his mouth and the other around his arms to keep him still. He was stronger than Max was, but Max tried desperately to kick him or anything that was in reach.

The guy brought him to the center of the room, away from anything Max could possibly knock over, and turned him to watch. On his bed, his backpack lifted into the air and turned itself over, dumping the contents out across his mess of blankets. It turned upright and opened. The pile of clean clothes his mother piled on the bed for him went into it.

Max went still while watching it. This wasn't happening. The acid had done something other than burn his leg. He never woke up this morning. Something else was happening right now. *Anything* else was happening.

His phone rang in his pocket. It went flying out the window a moment later.

He kept watching as the items from his bedside table went into his backpack. His Adderall, what was left of it, followed by his iPod. Water bottle. He wasn't seeing this.

Downstairs, the doorbell rang. Max snapped out of his daze. It didn't matter what he was seeing or if it was a hallucination or not. There was a guy who had broken into his house and he didn't want to know what his plans were. He needed to break free and call for help. That could be the police downstairs looking for this guy.

This guy might have been following him all day. Maybe that was why he felt like he was being watched.

Behind him, the guy stiffened and the backpack zipped itself up. He let go of Max's mouth and reached out, the backpack coming to his hand.

Max opened his mouth to yell for help, but his voice caught in his throat. His room vanished, turning into the dark outdoors. He dropped and the hand was back on his mouth again, Max struggling to find his footing. There was no footing here. They were in the tree outside his house and he was going to have a nasty fall if he struggled too much.

He stopped, instead watching his front door and trying to think of some way to get their attention without falling out of the tree. There had to be something he could do.

And then he saw who was there. The woman in white with two men in black suits.

"Hello," she said as his father answered the door. "I'm terribly sorry to be bothering you so late, but I'm actually here about your son. May I come in?"

"Why?" his father asked. He could see his mother appear in the doorway as well. "Has he done something?"

"Not yet. We think he might. We'd just like to talk to him and see for ourselves before it's too late."

"Too late for what?" his mother asked. "What's this about?"

"If you'd just let us in—"

"Do you have a warrant?"

The woman in white looked back at the men behind her. She gave them a small nod.

It was over a second later. Two gunshots rang in the night and his parents fell to the ground. The woman in white and her men walked over their bodies into the house.

The world fell out from under him.

CHAPTER THREE

MAX SAT UP so fast his head spun. There were words on the tip of his tongue, but they all tried to spill out at once. It came out as a jumbled yelp. He didn't even know which one to start with.

There was a strange kid in the house and he was dangerous.

Someone shot his parents.

He was being kidnapped.

He wasn't at home anymore. This wasn't the tree outside his house. It wasn't dark and he wasn't looking at the bodies of his parents in the doorway. He wasn't even lying sprawled out on the grass with a broken ankle from falling out of the tree.

He was in a guest room he'd never seen before. He sat on a queen sized bed covered in green blankets. There was a single, plain wooden dresser and a pile of boxes along one wall. A sewing machine was on the other with an open first aid kit next to it. Outside the window were the upper floors of a high rise building, some with people out on the balcony.

There was a door in the room. A girl sat there, her black hair tied back and she got slowly to her feet.

He patted his pocket. His phone was gone.

"Phone," he said, the single thought breaking through the mire of other panicking thoughts that were fighting inside his head. The words tumbled out with barely a break for a breath between. "Please, I need a phone. Someone broke into my house. I think they shot my parents. I was being kidnapped. There was this guy — I need to call the police."

She drew slowly closer to him. She looked about his age and some kind of Asian. He felt like he was looking at her in glimpses as the panic crept back in to take hold of his mind again. Her lips moved, but he had to focus before he could finally hear a word.

"Calm down," she said, firmly and sounding uncomfortable. She tried to keep herself composed, but Max could tell she was nervous, which did not help his panic. "It's okay. You're safe now. You're going to be all right."

"I need a phone," Max repeated. It was the only thing that made sense right now. "Police. My parents were shot."

"Deep breath," she said. She mimed a deep breath and kept doing it until Max repeated the action. He didn't feel any better. "My name is Allison. You can call me Ally."

"Hi Ally," Max said stiffly. "May I please use your phone?"

"I can't exactly—"

A small laugh from the sewing machine interrupted her. He snapped around to see a guy standing there where there had been no one a moment ago. He was a bit older than Max, with light wavy hair that looked like he'd just slept on it. He was at least six feet tall and his eyes settled on Max. "You won't need to call the police," he said, his voice gentle. "I'm sorry, but the police are already at your house. You need to stay with us for a while."

"Wh... I'm kidnapped aren't I?" Max asked, a fresh wave of panic washing over him.

"And that's my cue to go," he said. "I'll tell the others he's up."

He vanished from in front of the sewing machine. Max jumped and his heart raced. People weren't supposed to just vanish. They weren't supposed to move backpacks and clothes around without laying a hand on them either. They shouldn't be coming to his door late in the evening and shooting his parents. They shouldn't be putting him in a strange bed in some place that was surely several stories up. How did he even get here? How was any of this happening? Was this even real?

Ally scratched the back of her head and took a deep breath. She leaned over the bed and grabbed Max by the shoulders, forcing her to look at him. "You need to calm down," she told him. "Deep breaths. It's going to be okay."

She breathed deeply at him until he started to match her

breathing. Gradually, his heart settled back down in his chest and he relaxed. Ally let go of his shoulders, but kept eye contact with him and kept breathing with him until he let out a final long breath.

"You okay now?" she asked.

"Not even a little," Max told her. He was so confused and stressed that he could cry right now. He needed to focus on simple things for now. Little things that he could handle. One piece at a time. "Am I kidnapped? Are you going to keep me here?"

"No," Ally said. "This isn't a kidnapping. You're... you're one of us. You're safer if you stay with us."

"I've never even met you before," he said. He swung his legs off the far side of the bed away from her and got to his feet, feeling a little shaky. He made it to the window. He wanted to see just where he was for himself.

Outside was a city. There were high rises down the street, some office buildings and some other apartments. On the ground there were so many tiny people moving about on the sidewalks. Buses ran along the streets, at least three of them going either way at this moment below him.

Buses. He could hop a bus and figure out how to get back home.

When he was home he could call the cops.

Max ran for the door, hoping that he'd make it out of there

before anyone could stop him. He just needed to get to a bus and he could figure out how to get home from there. And get a phone. Someone would give him a phone down there.

Ally made one striking motion at the door and a wall of fire erupted from the ground. It flared up to the ceiling and surrounded the door. He fell back with a yell, falling hard on his ass and he could feel his hands shaking. This was getting to be too much. It was all just too much. His parents were dead, he was being followed and watched, someone had just disappeared and now there was a wall of fire.

"What's going on?" He could hear the desperation in his own voice, and the crack as he was starting to lose his handle on things. "What the fuck is happening?"

"Ally, what—"

Max's eyes met the vanishing guy's. He was back by the sewing machine again and he fell silent as he looked at Max. He let out a sigh and walked across the room, past Max to pat Ally gently on the shoulder. "Fine, I'll take this one," he said. "Maybe give Ted a hand downstairs?"

A wave of relief washed through Ally, her shoulders relaxing and the tension leaving her body. She placed her palms together and nodded to the guy before walking into the fire. When she left the room, she took the flames with her.

Max scrambled away while he had the chance, slipping under

the sewing table and pressing himself against the wall. He tried to breathe deep again to calm himself down, but his heart pounded so loudly in his ears and his hands were still shaking. He pressed them into the carpet to try and make them stop, but it did no good.

The guy approached him slowly and took a seat against the bed across from Max. He made no move to even lean forward and kept his hands on the ground next to him. He smiled at Max and Max got the distinct feeling that he was being treated like a scared puppy.

"My name's Harrison," the other guy said. "What's yours?"

"Max."

"Hi Max. I hate to break it to you, but you've just walked into an X-Men cartoon and you're going to be stuck here for a while."

"I really don't need anyone making fun of me right now," he muttered. He couldn't process anything that had just happened. He couldn't even figure out what kind of kidnapping this was. Couldn't they have just thrown him into a locked basement instead of having a couple people trying to be nice to him? A couple crazy people who did things that weren't possible outside of a cartoon. And one of them said he was one of them...

Harrison scratched at the back of his head. "At some point, all of us discovered we could do things. Weird things we couldn't explain. I can teleport. Ally does the fire thing. You saw. There's two more people downstairs. Jaime disappears. Ted tells terrible jokes."

Harrison smiled. Max's hands stopped shaking.

"Is there something you can do? Something you can't explain?"

Max's brain had moved from complete panic to numbness. There was too much to take in and try to process, so he stopped questioning any of it. He couldn't keep doing this. It all felt so real, but nothing about anything that was happening made any sense. He probably had actually fallen into an X-Men cartoon.

"Okay, let's get you up," Harrison said. He pulled Max out from under the table and got him to his feet. "There were some pills in your bag. Do you need to take those?"

If it was a cartoon, Max was probably the guy they introduced for one episode that was gone by the next. He'd probably be killed off to make the rest of the characters more determined to accomplish whatever their goals were.

"Max? Hey!"

"Huh?" Max blinked and turned to Harrison, then looked at the small pill bottle in his hand. He looked at it for a little longer before he recognized what it was and took it from him. "Right, I should take that."

"If you need some water I can..." Harrison offered, but Max took it dry and shoved the rest of the bottle into his pocket. "Are those really important things we should know about?"

"What?" Max reached into his pocket and took the pills out again, looking at them. "It's just Adderall," he said. Harrison didn't ask anything else, so he put them back in his pocket.

"So can you do anything weird?" Harrison asked.

"I don't..."

"It's okay if you can't," he said, leading him out the door to the rest of the building. "You'll find out what it is, probably sooner than later. Funny thing is whenever someone new shows up, we all get a little stronger at what we do. That's why we're all living together right now. Strength in numbers."

That sounded rehearsed, but Max decided not to call him on it. He was taking him out of the room. Out of the room was good. "I really don't want to talk about the superpowers thing right now," he said.

They stopped outside in the crimson hall. There were rooms on either side, each with a closed white door blocking his view. On the walls were pictures of a family of six with kids ranging from elementary to high school.

"No problem," Harrison said. "I'll give you the tour instead. We can talk about whatever you want."

"I want to know what happened," he said. "Some guy breaks

into my house, does all this weird shit, drags me outside to watch a bunch of guys in suits shoot my parents after they were asking about me. I mean, why would they even want me? And why bother with my parents at all? There's plenty of chance to get me on my own tomorrow. Or today? What day is it?"

"I'm sorry about your parents," Harrison said. "Really. But the police are already there taking care of it and... just trust me, you don't want to go home right now. It's a bad idea. Trust me."

Max said nothing. He blocked out the image of his parents lying lifeless on the ground and tried not to think about it. He just needed to get back home. He could get answers if he went back. People would be worried about him. Jeremy would probably be freaking out.

"Luke, by the way," Harrison said. "That's the guy who went to get you. And it wasn't kidnapping, exactly. He just needed to get you out of there before the other guys showed up to take you themselves."

"He could have said something."

Harrison hesitated. "He can't actually," he said. "Near as we can tell, both Luke and Willow can't actually talk. Ally's been trying to teach them sign language, but you've seen how good she is with patience."

"She's tried to set them on fire?"

"I promise, this stuff does get easier to deal with," Harrison told him. "Kind of. Once you figure out what you can do, you'll be golden."

"Golden? Do people really say that?"

He smiled. Max did too. "Well, Max," Harrison said, "I guess you're ready to know the basics of travelling with us since you're going to be stuck with us for a while. We tend to move around a lot, almost weekly, so don't get too used to that bed. We stay in empty houses, mostly people who are on vacation, and eat all their food. Luke and Willow have the final say on whether we stay or go anywhere. The more we move around, the harder it is to track us down and they always seem to know when someone is after us. If you want to leave, you're free to at any time, but go with a buddy."

"Okay?" Max didn't follow most of that, but nodded and pretended he did. He would leave tonight, anyway, as soon as everyone was asleep and he could slip out. He could catch a bus and figure out how to get back home.

"We're going to go meet everyone. You think you're okay to do that?"

Max nodded and followed Harrison down the hallway.

"Jeremy's probably freaking out," Max said.

"Who?"

"Friend. I was on voice with him when Luke broke into my room."

"Try not to think about home," he said, sounding a little sad. "It's not going to help. Come on, they're just downstairs."

CHAPTER FOUR

HE COULD SEE most of the lower floor from the top of the stairs. There were windows covering one wall, reminding Max again just how far up he was. There was a dining room at the bottom of the stairs and a kitchen to the right with Ally and another guy moving around inside it. To the left of it, he could see the back of a couch and the familiar faint glow of a television lighting a darker room.

The dining room was empty except for two people sitting in the bench of the window moving their hands furiously at one another. He didn't know who the girl who looked like a goth maid was. Her dark hair was pulled back into two pigtails and she kept moving her gloved hands in small, sharp gestures. Max wondered if she remembered how to smile.

The other was the one that kidnapped him.

He stopped where he was on the stairs. Luke. His name was Luke and he looked just the same as he did last night. Dark clothes, tinged with red, and his dark hair was a mess. He had deep circles under his eyes, but he kept a gentle smile on his face as Willow continued to gesture madly at him, occasionally moving his hands in response.

"Come on," Harrison said gently, pushing him forward. "They aren't going to hurt you. Well, Willow might. Don't piss her off if you can help it, trust me. You want her on your side if a fight ever breaks out."

Max let Harrison lead him down the stairs. Luke looked over when they reached the bottom and nodded, but made no other move. Willow ignored them both.

The door out of this place was a room away behind the stairs. As soon as he thought he could make a break for it, he was getting out of here. For now, he just needed to play along.

"Over this way," Harrison said, leading him over to a modern looking kitchen full of stainless steel appliances and a distinct lack of walls separating it from anything else. Ally looked up from the peppers and put down the knife. That would make the black guy with the short dreads standing at the sink…

"You know Ally. This is Ted."

"Hey," Ted said, turning away from the fruit and letting the water run over it. Max noticed that the water completely left his hands as soon as he pulled them out of the sink. He reached over the island in the middle of the kitchen and extended a hand to Max. "Done freaking out?"

He was getting out of here tonight. Home didn't have any of whatever this stuff happening was.

"Not quite," Max admitted, taking his hand and shaking it. "I'm Max."

"Don't worry about it, Max," he said. "Not everyone gets used to this stuff as easily as I do."

"You mean crying in the corner for a week?" Ally asked.

"Tear bending," Ted corrected him. "It is a time honoured tradition of the water tribe."

"Avatar?" Max asked.

"Finally someone knows what I'm talking about!" Ted said. "You need to see them, Ally. You'll love them. They're practically anime."

"I'm not even Japanese!"

"Thailand's close, right?"

"I was born in Phoenix."

"Let's keep going," Harrison said. He led Max back through the dining room, Luke and Willow no longer sitting in the bay window or anywhere to be seen at all. "The only one left is Jaime. She doesn't really talk much, though."

Max stayed quiet and followed to a living room with a large television hung up on the wall. CSI: Miami was playing through a layer of static, the music sting telling him what was actually happening on the screen more than anything. The DVD cases lay open on the floor in front of the television.

Sitting with her feet up on the reclining chair next to the couch was a kid Max was sure was barely old enough to be in middle school. She wore a knit cap that covered her short, unevenly cut hair and long pants with several pockets. She kept her arms crossed and eyes firmly on the screen.

"Jaime," Harrison said. "New kid. His name's Max."

"Hey," Jaime said, not looking away from the screen. "Can you change the disc?"

Harrison clapped Max on the shoulder. "I'm going to go help with dinner. You going to be okay?"

Max nodded and watched him go. He thought about running right there, but they could see the door better from the kitchen. Harrison could stop him pretty easily. They could have this door rigged like the one upstairs.

He went to the DVDs on the ground and switched the disc. Jaime, with remote in hand, started the first episode. Max sat down on the couch far away from her and watched it through the static, wondering just how anyone could afford a place like this and have such crappy television quality.

Once night fell and everyone went to sleep, then he'd get out of here. With this quality television, he didn't imagine they'd have reason to stay awake long. The street outside looked like it was in some city somewhere, so they should have late night buses. He just needed to find change.

He could tell Jaime kept looking at him, but tried not to look back. He just learned that the main character was the one with the sunglasses that people made that meme out of.

"How's the lady in white?" Jaime asked after the first episode ended.

"What?"

Jaime didn't repeat herself, instead looking Max over like she was trying to decide what to think of him. "You like CSI?"

"Never seen it before," he said. The next episode was starting, but it didn't seem like a show he really needed to pay attention to. "Who names their kid Horatio Kane?"

Max didn't know what to make of the look Jaime gave him at that. She looked almost offended that he would ask that at all.

Max got up and left rather than deal with whatever he'd said. He looked longingly at the door as he got to the dining room, then to the three who were now assembling plates of food in the kitchen. Whatever it was, it smelled good, but he was careful to stay on the far side of the breakfast bar instead of going into the kitchen.

"Hey," Harrison said, passing him a plate. "Did you get the TV working?"

Max didn't answer, too distracted by the food that he'd just been handed. It looked like someone had made a full Thanksgiving dinner with beef instead of turkey. It smelled as good as it looked and the reminded him of just how long it probably was since he last ate. Harrison passed him a knife and fork and nodded for him to start eating.

It looked a little too good to not be poisoned.

"I'm gonna go stare at the static," Ted said, grabbing a second plate. "You guys clean up."

Harrison took a seat next to him at the bar and started in on his own plate. Max poked at his. He was so hungry and Harrison looked like he was fine. He tried a small bite first, finding that nothing about it tasted wrong. With food in front of him, he was starving. Maybe it would be all right.

They ate in silence for a while before Max started to feel awkward about it. "What's up with the television?" he asked, needing to fill the silence somehow.

"That's nothing," Ally told him, fixing herself a plate as she talked. "You should hear the phones. Static."

"It's mostly because of us," Harrison said. "We tend to screw up the electronic devices everywhere we end up. I haven't been able to get to get online in, like, months."

"No Facebook," Ally said almost automatically, longing lacing her words. "No internet. God, television barely works wherever we go. Cable scrambles, satellite stops working, the *phones* on a land line don't even work."

She sat down with her plate on Max's other side. Surrounded, he tried to keep his glances at the door to a minimum.

"How are you settling in so far?" Ally asked.

Max shrugged. "Okay."

"Which means still freaking out," Harrison said. "It's okay. You'll get used to it eventually. I mean, it took Ted a couple weeks."

"It didn't take you that long," Ally said to Harrison. "You were good after a couple days."

"That was a bit of a special case," Harrison said. "And I was still freaking out for a while after that."

"How long have you been doing this?" Max asked through a mouthful of mashed potatoes.

"I've been here for six or seven months I guess?" Harrison said, looking at Ally. "Ally's been around for... what? A year now? And Jaime's been here even longer?"

"Really? She looks like she's still a kid."

"She was already travelling with Luke and Willow when they rescued me," Ally told him. "There used to be others, but they were caught by the White Woman or the Lady in White and the Men in Black or whatever we're calling them now. Jaime doesn't talk about it and, well, Luke and Willow *can't* talk about it."

"Because they're mute?"

"Because both of them completely *refuse* to learn sign language," Ally said. "Like, I actually know it. I have tried to teach them so many times, but nothing. You'd think they'd want to tell us what's going on when they disappear all the time or give us a heads up when we're about to move, but *no*."

"Don't be fooled," Harrison said. "She still keeps trying to teach them every chance she can."

"Definition of madness," she muttered, shaking her head and shoving a few vegetables into her mouth.

Max stayed quiet, his eyes risking another look at the front door. They'd been here months and years. If he didn't get out of here soon, he was worried he'd never be able to leave.

CHAPTER FIVE

THE TWO FLOOR apartment they took refuge in was only five floors up and did not have a door rigged to shoot fire at him when he tried to open it. With everyone asleep by ten, it was easy to just wait a couple more hours to be sure they stayed asleep, walk out the door and take the elevator down to the lobby, past the doorman who smiled pleasantly at him, and out the front door. It was so easy that he wondered what the catch was.

It was a cool, cloudy night with no traffic. He didn't think a city could ever be quite as quiet as it was, but he didn't let it bother him. He kept walking until he found a bus stop just in sight of the apartment to sit down at. They were asleep, but he didn't want to miss a light switch on and let them catch him unaware just as a bus was coming. The sign on this one said that he'd just missed the midnight bus and it would be another hour before he could catch another.

Max settled down on the bench and started going through

his backpack. Despite it being emptied out, he managed to find change in a couple of the pockets and put together what should be enough bus fare to get him close to home. He could at least get far away from here and maybe find a police officer who could help him figure out how to get the rest of the way.

Maybe the police would drive by now and he could flag them down.

He didn't stop at change and kept looking through the pockets for more money. He had no idea where he was or how far it was to get home, but if he needed to, he could probably sell his iPod for a ticket to get the rest of the way. Once he was there, he could probably stay with Tara or Jeremy while the police dealt with whatever happened at his house. Maybe his parents survived, but his house would probably still be taped off. Even if he was stuck on a couch for a while, he would much rather be home than in that apartment.

Everyone up there seemed nice enough, but he had no idea what was going on. Not only had all these people decided to stay with the ones who had kidnapped them for months to years, but there was something else happening. His eyes were playing tricks on him or the panic from being kidnapped in the first place was screwing with his head, but there was something going on up there that he didn't understand. At the very least, he knew that no one there owned that place.

He glanced up at the apartment, looking for any lights on. Maybe they would just let him leave. They didn't seem like bad people. He didn't know what was wrong with them, but they all seemed decent enough.

"Didn't I tell you about the travelling in pairs thing?"

Max jumped clear off the bench and fell hard on the ground. Harrison looked amused and offered him a hand up. Max hesitated and got up on his own. Max took another step away from Harrison, just out of his arm's reach, and looked down the street to see if the bus was coming. Maybe he could just jump on.

"Are you going to take me back?" he asked, hoping to see the headlights of the bus coming around the corner.

"Nope," Harrison said, plopping down on the end of the bench away from Max, looking pleased with himself. "If you want to hop the bus and get out of here, I'm not stopping you. Even brought change if you need it. I am going to try and talk you out of it, though."

Max exhaled and took a seat on the opposite end of the bench, as far away from Harrison as he could. That was fine. Something told him that he wasn't lying to him about anything but the change. Harrison would actually let him go and, looking around the empty street, Max figured he could use the company to pass the time. "What do you think is going to convince me to stay with some guy who kidnapped me?"

Harrison laughed. "Max, I can go wherever I want. Literally. When Luke first got to me, do you really think I didn't immediately try to get home? I wanted to know what happened and I slipped out and went back to see. Luke followed along when I did, but he didn't stop me. He just kind of... hung back and let me see for myself."

Harrison hesitated a moment, Max still not sure what to make of it. "It was a week later, I guess," Harrison said. "The tape was still up at my house. No one was there when I went in, but no one had cleaned up yet either. There's a lot less blood than you'd think from getting shot in the head, apparently. It was a mess. Nothing had been moved. Their bodies weren't there, but there was the chalk outline. I could almost see them lying there. They killed my mom and my sister."

Harrison went quiet for a moment. Max stayed still, not knowing how to react or if Harrison even remembered he was there. Finally, Harrison let out a breath and shook his head.

"I knew they were dead, but I thought that maybe I could still go back. You know, maybe they weren't dead and hope that maybe everything would work out alright. Luke wasn't all that keen on it, but I thought that maybe I could just go check out the police station. You know, walk in, say who I was and I had information on the people who killed my parents? Seemed like something that might work. They could help me get back on my feet after all that."

Max listened intently. Harrison was following his plan exactly and, as far as Max could tell, he wasn't lying.

"The police station was a bad idea. It seems like a good idea, but it's a bad idea. If you go back, don't do it. It went fine at first. You walk in, you try to think of what you're going to say. You're nervous and you look over the walls. All the faces. And then you see your face in a photo, an old one that they just pulled out of somewhere. You look terrible in it, and it's weird to see yourself on the wall. And then you read the rest of the paper it's printed on and you find out that you're wanted for murder. And you panic. And you run. You get as far away as you can, until... Well, I don't know when you stop."

Harrison gave him a half hearted smile. "And then I got caught by a couple guys in suits. The people who killed my parents, they wanted me alive apparently. Luke saved me and got me back to the safe house. Men in suits, that woman in white, they keep coming after us when we leave for too long. That's why I'm here still."

Max wasn't sure what to say to that. There wasn't much he could say. He wasn't ready to accept it as a possibility, and he glanced over for the headlights. Harrison wasn't lying, but he couldn't accept that it would happen to him.

"Ally insisted on going back too, apparently," he said. "Jaime said she didn't take it well either. I was pissed that she didn't warn me about it, but she didn't think telling me would make a difference."

"And you think you can talk me out of it?"

"Not really," he admitted. "We always tend to go against our better judgement in these cases, you know? It's your family. You have to see it for yourself. Just be careful out there. You're probably suspect number one and you might want to try to keep away from the police for a little while. Lie low. Stay with people who you know will hide you."

"I'll keep that in..." he started, but there was that feeling again. Like there was someone was looking for him him. He had no idea what it was, but it was strong. He looked around and looked back at Harrison, who seemed a little concerned himself.

"You okay?"

"Fine," Max said a little too quickly. "Fine, just a little tired."

"You sure?" he asked. "Maybe your powers are just kicking in."

"I still can't believe this superpowers thing," Max admitted, glad for a change in subject. "I mean, when did my life stop making sense? Two days ago everything was completely normal, then yesterday, Luke. And today you, Ally, everything."

"It's a little overwhelming," Harrison said, smiling. "Just wait until you start, I don't know, blowing things up with your mind or something."

"Don't you already have Ally for that?"

"True," he said. "It's not that cute when she does it."

Max let out a nervous laugh. That feeling wasn't going away. "So what's the deal with them? The superpowers. Do you use them and learn and master them until you become the ultimate teleporter ever or what?"

"Not exactly," Harrison said. "Ted's figured out how to get better with them, but it's weird. Ally noticed that we get stronger with them the more people join the group. I can teleport farther now and carry more people with me now that Ted's around."

"Really?"

Harrison shrugged. "I think so. Ally's noticed it more than I have. Every time someone new joins, we seem to get a bit of a power boost. Not that we get any better with them. Well, Ted can help you get better, but it means hanging out with Ted."

"He doesn't seem that bad."

"I have no idea what he's talking about half the time."

Max couldn't argue with that, smiling a little and letting it all drop for now. Ted referencing Avatar earlier gave Max an idea of where his pop culture references might come from and Harrison didn't seem like the type that would recognize any of them.

He looked back down the street for the bus again. He felt anxious. The thing looking for him felt like it was getting closer and this time, it didn't seem like whatever it was would stop at just finding Max. He was starting to feel the urge to run himself.

"You should go," Max said. Whatever it was that was coming, if anything was coming at all, it was almost here. If nothing was coming, he wasn't going to let Harrison know that he was getting paranoid over nothing. "I think the bus is almost here. There's no need to stick around and wait with me."

"It's fine," Harrison said, relaxing on the bench. "Sometimes I need a break from in there. Only time I usually leave is to go on runs with Jaime and her ankle's busted so I've been cooped up in there for way too long."

"Is that Jaime's problem?"

"Nope. She's always like that. Seriously, are you okay?"

Max tried to keep himself from looking as nervous as he felt. Whatever it was, it was getting closer. He felt like running, given that last time his day had ended with tragedy and ending up here. It could have been a coincidence last time, but if it wasn't...

"I'm fine," he said. There was nothing coming. Nothing but the bus. And he was going to get on it and head home to figure things out. He was going to be fine and he would go home. Home. Just focus on getting home. "Really, I'm—"

Harrison jumped to his feet and charged him, fist pulled back and ready to strike. He turned to run, but someone stood behind him. He stumbled around the other man and tripped. The other man, wearing a black suit and sunglasses, caught him on his way down.

There was a yell of pain and Max looked over. Harrison fell back to the ground on the other side of a wall of fire, clutching his arm.

Max twisted out of the other man's grasp, falling back on the ground. He looked up at a man dressed in a black suit and wearing dark glasses in the middle of the night. He scooted backwards on the ground, his hands scraping against the concrete and tried to scramble to his feet without letting his eyes leave the other person. He fell off the curb hard and onto the street, his elbows taking the brunt of the fall. His eyes darted down the street, hoping this time not to see anything coming to run him over.

The man in the suit turned to him, the wall of fire appearing behind Max, blocking his escape route. He could feel the fire licking at his back. His arm was warm and he saw his sleeve on fire. With a yelp, he madly patted out the flames with his hand. The man lunged forward to grab him and Max stepped back into the fire.

And then he was gone, the fire wall dissipating with him. Max fell back onto the road and he looked around, finding the suited man stumbling backwards a few feet away. Willow walked towards the man, her red eyes narrowed.

Harrison got up, his arm held close and looking much worse for wear as he stumbled over to Max.

The man rose a hand towards Max, but Harrison got in the way. The man closed his hand and jerked it backwards, pulling Harrison down to the ground and back towards him. Willow stepped in, grabbing the bus pole from the ground and tearing it out as if it was nothing. She threw it at him, knocking the man backwards. Harrison stopped skidding along the concrete, groaning and staying very still.

Max looked back at Willow, her eyes still on the man. He turned his attention to her, throwing the bus stop sign back onto the street to keep it from hitting himself. With the two of them distracted, Max went over to Harrison and tried to get him up, pulling his good arm over his shoulder and bringing him to his feet.

"Come on," he said, trying to be comforting despite his panic. "We gotta get out of here."

"Yeah," Harrison said, grimacing. He looked up to the window. "Hold tight."

CHAPTER SIX

MAX DID NOT try to question how they were back in the apartment a moment later. He felt Harrison go limp over his shoulders as soon as they were back in the apartment and Max was trying to keep from freaking out over everything that had happened.

Processing whatever happened outside would have to wait. For now, he needed to get Harrison down off his shoulders. The couch was next to him, but there was someone already there.

"Jaime!" Max said, a bit more sharply than he intended. Jaime woke with a start, but she was alert enough to get off the couch so Max could put Harrison down. "Get Luke. Willow's down on the street fighting some guy in a suit and—"

Jaime was gone as soon as he said that much, though she moved slowly and hobbled when she walked. Injured ankle. Harrison mentioned that.

Max turned to Harrison who was now bleeding on the couch.

He turned on the lights to take a better look, finding that the scratches on him were mostly superficial. Bleeding, maybe with a little asphalt in them, but it wasn't anything serious. The thing that was giving him the most trouble was his arm, blistering and clearly burned very badly.

He looked up to see Ally standing there, curious and trying to figure out what was going on. "Jaime said—"

"First aid kit," Max said. "There's one upstairs. And anything you have for burns."

"Yeah. Sure."

Ally left and Max took a deep breath. Did he even learn anything about burns? First aid was part of his lifeguard training, but he couldn't remember if he'd done that part already or if he was supposed to be doing that later. He hoped he'd already done it and it would come to him.

Ally came back less than a minute later with the kit in hand. She gave it to Max, looking worriedly between him and Harrison. Harrison looked haggard, right on the edge of consciousness.

"Talk to him," Max said, taking a look through the kit for something that might help. It looked expensive, at least, but it was organized poorly and he was having trouble finding the right materials to deal with a burn. There was more in here than the kits he saw when he was studying.

Ally rushed over to Harrison's side, looking torn between

wanting to smack him and console him for his recklessness. "What the hell happened?"

Harrison stirred, eyes refocusing. He grimaced as he shifted his arm. He pulled it just a little away from his body to get a better look, a stain of blood on his shirt. Immediately, he put it back down and looked like he was going to be sick. "You know how I yelled at you for not warning me about what happens when you go back home?" he asked.

"That doesn't mean you go and be a hero," she scolded him. "It means you warn him *before he leaves*."

"Got it," Max muttered, finally pulling out the right pieces. A sterile cloth already soaked in burn ointment, which should work alright, and gauze that he could use to keep it in place. Cloths for cleaning. He took another breath and tried to keep his hands steady. "This is probably going to hurt," he told Harrison before he started cleaning the bits of concrete out of his skin and wrapping his arm.

Harrison gritted his teeth and tried not to make a sound as he worked, though he did a miserable job of it, groans and yelps of pain escaping his lips while Max did his best to be gentle. His fingers twitched with almost every movement Max made which, while they were pain movements, struck Max as a good sign. At least his hand was still working.

A gunshot rang outside. None of them even looked up.

"How did you even do this to yourself?" Ally demanded, bringing his attention back to her while Max worked. "You burned yourself just *talking*?"

"One of the men in black showed up," Harrison said, his voice pained, though he was making an effort to keep his composure. He let out another yelp as Max went over one of the blisters. "Apparently they don't like it when you try to punch them in the face."

"You punched him?"

"Tried to," he corrected her. "I didn't quite get far enough before I realized my arm was on fire. And then he dragged me across the concrete. I think I hit my head."

"Do you feel dizzy at all?" Max asked absently, now wrapping his arm with gauze.

"I don't know," he said. "I only really feel my arm right now and *that* feels like shit."

"That should do it," Max said, finishing the loose bandaging and backing away. He looked through the medical kit. There should at least be something in here for the pain, since that had to be killing him. Right now he was probably working on adrenaline and Max had to admit he was still feeling the thrill of it as well.

Ally was at a loss for words. "You're an idiot." She turned on Max as well. "Both of you! What the hell did *you* do?"

"What?" he asked, looking down to where she was looking. He

could see the burn marks on his black hoodie from where it had been on fire. "Right, probably shouldn't keep wearing this."

His hands were starting to shake again, but he forced them still and tore off the hoodie, throwing it into a corner and going back to the kit. Should he really be giving a burn victim anything that also qualified as a blood thinner? He definitely had to answer that on a test once.

"Hey Max?" Harrison asked weakly from the couch.

"Hm?" Max asked, still going through the kit and not turning around. One of these should work.

"How can you not feel that, you dumbass?" Ally demanded.

Max turned back, confused. He looked to Ally, who gestured at his elbow. He looked at it, noticing now there was a little blood dripping off of it. It was burned fairly badly, but he could still move it for now. He barely felt it, though that was probably the adrenaline. "Huh."

"*Huh*?" she demanded. "That's all you have to say?"

"Can you give me a hand?" he asked. "I think one of these sterile pads should be big enough to cover it."

He handed it to her and she hesitated before taking it and opening it. "I swear to god, you're both idiots," Ally muttered as she carefully applied it to his arm. "You *don't leave* without someone else. This is why you don't leave on your own."

He looked up at the house around them to find that the ceiling was much lower. The couch had changed. The television had even changed. He couldn't see the kitchen anymore.

"Hey?" Max asked. "Are we in a different house?"

CHAPTER SEVEN

THE CITY OUTSIDE was gone. The street was gone. The bus stop was gone.

Harrison lay on the couch. Max went looking for the washroom and when he came back, Ally was panicking. Harrison had thrown up and passed out. Someone cleaned it up. It might have been him. Ally went away and didn't come back after that. Jaime didn't return to this different living room. Max wasn't sure she even made it to the new house.

His mind buzzed with guilt mixed in with thoughts he didn't want to process. Crazy though it sounded, he knew that something was coming for him. He knew it twice now. He should have made Harrison leave and tried to get out of there on his own. He should have gone further away so no one could find him. He should have gone back inside and tried again the next night. He should have done *something*.

He didn't even see Willow or Luke come by. He sat against

the wall behind the open medical kit and watched Harrison, chest slowly rising and falling. They should get him to a hospital, but Max doubted he could even stand right now. He felt sick from just the memory of Harrison's burnt arm and the guilt of it happening because of him. He only wanted to help and this was what he'd gotten.

It was a crazy sort of help, but Max had to wonder how much of it was true. The teleporting, the men in black, not to mention the fire! He couldn't think of any way to explain it and he knew he could feel someone coming. At this point, powers were not the strangest thing that could happen to him.

And then there was that story. If he went home and found out that he was wanted for what happened that night...

He just wanted Harrison to be all right.

Max couldn't keep his hands from shaking now that he wasn't doing anything with them. He couldn't process everything. This wasn't reality. This was a movie that he'd just walked into — one where he could still feel pain. He hadn't even felt how badly burnt he was. He still couldn't even feel it.

Is this what shock feels like?

Jaime tripped over him the next morning on her way back to the couch, jostling him out of his sleep. Max scrambled up and watched Jaime as she tried to keep her feet. She shifted to keep most of her weight on her left foot and hobbled to the L shaped couch. She dropped onto it and looked at Harrison as she put her feet up on the coffee table.

Max looked at Harrison too. He was tired, but seeing the gentle rise and fall of Harrison's chest was comforting. At least he wasn't dead yet.

"He gonna be okay?" Jaime asked, her eyes carefully looking over Harrison.

Max hesitated. He knew he was supposed to say yes, but he was too tired to sound convincing. "He *should* be in the hospital," Max told her. "He said he's wanted for murder, though, so I don't know what you guys do about that."

"He'll get better, though?"

Harrison didn't look like he was in any discomfort while he slept. He was breathing in a steady rhythm. Max didn't want to go over and see just how bad the burns under the bandages were, though. He could still smell a bit of the vomit from the previous night and worried he might add to it if he looked at his broiled arm without panic and adrenaline fueling him.

He needed a hospital.

Max let his eyes wander back over to Jaime and the feet she had up on the table. Neither were wrapped, but her right ankle had swollen to twice the size of her left. "You should wrap that at least," Max said, turning to the open medical kit. He removed a roll of tensor bandages. "And ice it if there's any."

Jaime flinched as Max reached across the coffee table and started to feel the bones to try and tell if it was broken. He couldn't quite tell under the swelling and the reds, purples and yellows caused by the bruising. He wasn't sure how much of that was a result of Jaime continuing to move on it. It felt like she might have a small fracture. "How does it feel when I…"

Max looked up to find Jaime completely stiff on the couch. Max let go of her foot and backed off to the other side of the table. "Sorry, I just — If it's *broken* then maybe… I'm sorry."

Jaime let out a grunt and kicked the tensor bandages toward him, followed by placing her foot further across the table easier access. She didn't make eye contact, instead taking up the remote and turning on the television to surf through the static.

Max wrapped up the ankle, trying to make sure it was secure enough that she wouldn't be able to move it but not so much that he might damage something if there was anything seriously wrong with it. He might need to splint it to keep it from getting any worse.

Both of them needed to see a proper doctor. There was only so much he could do with what little first aid he knew. He wasn't even fully finished with the course yet. They still had to learn to deal with things like neck injuries and, given everything that had happened in the less than twenty four hours he'd been there, he wasn't ruling that out as a possibility.

He should call an ambulance. Get both of them out of here. Maybe he'd go too. Maybe the cops would realize that Harrison hadn't killed his family and it would all work out.

Jaime scratched the back of her head absently as Max finished, her brow furrowing as she looked down at her ankle. She nodded when Max pulled away.

"You should stay off it for a while," Max said, getting to his feet. "I'll see if I can find some ice or something for the swelling."

"What about you?" he asked.

Max turned back, then followed Jaime's eyes to his arm. The bandage covering his elbow and up the back of his arm had turned brown overnight from the blood seeping through it. It didn't hurt to move it and he couldn't feel anything at all from it besides it being a bit uncomfortable.

"I should change that," Max said, grabbing another bandage from the kit. "I'll be back with ice."

Max got to his feet and felt the blood rush away from his head. He stumbled out of the room, leaning against the wall as he made his way down the narrow hall. Of course he was tired. He'd barely slept, and what little sleeping he'd done, he was lying on the ground. He was still exhausted.

It helped that this house was made of narrow hallways with doors everywhere. He opened them to a study, a closet and a storage room before he found the washroom door open at the end of the hall.

He ran the water and washed his face, looking up at his reflection in the mirror. He looked as awful as he felt. His hair was matted down in his face and it looked like he hadn't slept in a week. Maybe he'd find a bed after he got the ice for Jaime. First, though, he needed to fix himself up.

The bandage was on his arm firmly. He managed to peel away a corner of it, pulling the hair on his arm away with it, and got it half off before he stopped.

Under the red and brown blood, there was no sign of a blister or even a cut. He was perfectly fine.

He brushed the bandage back up his arm, setting it back in place as if he'd never taken it off in the first place. He could deal with that later.

He took an Adderall and went looking for the kitchen.

The kitchen was easy enough to find. The smell of bacon wafted down the stairs, leading Max up to the second floor where Ted was at the stove and Ally had a smoothie in each hand. She put them down on the kitchen table as soon as she saw Max.

"Who're those for?" Max asked, pointing at the drinks. "Luke and Willow. Is he awake?" she asked.

"You look like shit, dude," Ted said, turning around to look at him. "Did you sleep?"

"Is Harrison awake?" Ally asked again.

Max blinked at her. He was only getting more tired the more he kept moving. "Not yet. He might be out for a while. He needs a doctor."

"We can't," she told him. "We're wanted. We can't just go to the hospital."

"Then you just gotta wait," he said. "Is there any ice? Jaime really needs it for her ankle."

"You look like you need to lie down," Ted said. "You okay?"

"I'll get the ice," Ally said, pushing Max to the table. "Jaime's keeping an eye on Harrison, then?"

"Yeah. Something like that."

"Harrison's name ain't Logan," Ted told her. "He's not going to be better after a couple hours. We might have to break the no authorities rule on this one."

Max was aware of the tension in the room as Ally gathered up a bag of ice and left without another word. He couldn't bring himself to pay any attention to it, his eyes insisting on drooping closed. He probably should just find a bed to crash in, but everyone else seemed to be up and moving. He didn't want to be the only one asleep in a house of people he barely knew.

"Sounds like I missed a party last night," Ted said. "It's always a little weird waking up in a different house than you went to sleep in when you didn't have anything to drink night before."

Max couldn't bring himself to pay much attention to anything else Ted said, the fatigue wearing him down. Even the table with its plastic place mats looked comfortable right now. The table got closer and he put his head down on it, arm hanging loose at his side. Rest. He only needed a few minutes rest.

CHAPTER EIGHT

MAX WOKE TO something being torn off his arm. He let out a yelp of pain and banged his arm into the table as he pulled it away. He held it across his body, his hand nursing his elbow.

"Don't touch it!" Ally yelled at him. "It's probably still open!"

"What the hell are you doing?" Max demanded.

"I told you to leave him alone," Ted said, rolling his eyes and pushing Ally over to the sink. "Dishes. Max, give me a hand and show me where the sick bay is?"

Ted handed Max a single plate and glass of juice before picking up two plates, a bowl and several cups himself. Max shot a glare at Ally before leading the way downstairs, going slowly so that Ted could keep up and keep his balance.

At least, that's what he told himself. The truth was he still felt drained.

"I hear you tried to leave last night," Ted said. "Hey, it's probably better that you didn't get that far. It's not like any of us really have a home to go back to anymore."

"I don't know what happened," Max said. "Some guy in a suit and glasses showed up and everything went a little crazy. There was fire and I don't even know what was going on until Willow showed up. Harrison got us out of there and then we were back here again."

"You mean the last here," Ted corrected. "This here showed up about half way through the night."

"Yeah, that," Max said. This whole thing was making his head hurt and he really needed to sleep.

"You should have tried punching him. Who knows, maybe it's your thing."

"What's your thing?"

"Hold up," Ted said, stopping them in the hall. A small stream of water came out one of the glasses in his hands, free of the orange juice in the rest of the cup. "Water," he said, the water falling back into the cup. "Not as flashy as setting things on fire, but you can do a lot with it. Never have to worry about getting soaked in the rain again. Don't sweat. Always have a drink when you need it. And check this out."

He looked at the cup in Max's hands and narrowed his eyes at it. Max looked too and watched as three distinct lumps of ice appeared. "I have been trying to figure out how to turn it to ice for a week and yesterday, it just starts working! Can't get them off the ground yet, but I can get them moving around a little."

The ice cubes danced around in the glass for a moment before they dissolved back into water. He shook his head and looked a little tired from the effort. "I need a little more practice, but I should be able to get it soon. Pretty cool, huh?"

"You're going to show me how to do that, right?" Max asked.

"If I can," Ted said. "All depends on what you can do. Pointless showing you how to move water around if you're moving things with your mind, you know. Still, I managed to teach Ally a thing or two."

Max stifled a yawn and started back to the living room where Jaime and Harrison were holed up.

"Hey, until we figure out what you do, at least you know first aid, right? That should come in handy around here. You could probably look in on whatever happened to Luke and Willow last night."

"What happened? I mean, to them. I thought they were invincible or something."

"Ally said Luke got hurt or something. She got a glimpse in when she dropped them breakfast. They're holed up in one of the rooms upstairs."

"Yeah, maybe later."

"No one's going to be mad because you tried to leave, dude,"

Ted told him as they entered the living room. "Everyone's tried to leave. *Everyone.* I think."

"Aren't you the last person to show up before me?"

Ted didn't say anything, setting the dishes down on the coffee table in the middle of the room. Jaime leaned over to grab a plate and Ted put the bowl of oatmeal on the table by Harrison, still sleeping. He grabbed his own plate and started in on it, ignoring the daytime television that Jaime was watching through more light static.

Max started in on his, but his eye caught on Jaime's ankle resting on the table, now with a melted bag of water on it. "You shouldn't leave that on for too long," Max told her, pointing at the water.

Jaime tilted her leg and the bag fell off along with the towel it was resting on. Underneath it, her ankle was considerably less swollen already. The bandages looked loose on her now. Max tried not to keep looking at it as he ate his plate of bacon and eggs. He felt better and more alert with every bite.

"So is he gonna be okay?" Ted asked, keeping his voice low.

"Why do you guys keep asking me?" Max asked. "I don't know. I've never seen anything like that before."

"How bad was it?"

"I don't know, it's—"

A soft groan stopped him. He looked over to Harrison as he stirred, his good hand coming up over his face and his eyes opening. His head fell to the side, looking at the two of them, then up around the room. "Different house?" he asked.

"So you *are* going to live," Ted said. "Ally thinks you're dying."

"I might still be dying. Why does it smell like vomit?"

"Oh, thank god," Ally said, appearing in the door and going to his side. She tried to help him up, sitting next to him and minding every groan and wince of pain as he moved until he was upright. Once he was up, she handed him the bowl of oatmeal. "How are you feeling? How's your arm?"

Harrison looked down at the bowl in his hand, pondering the spoon. "Sore," he said. He put the bowl down on the table and looked to the bandages on his arm. They were soaked through, but he wasn't bothered by it. "You know, this looks a lot worse than it actually feels."

"We should probably change that," Ally said. "You eat. I'll check and see if there's enough left over."

She got up and went to the medical kit as Harrison started on the oatmeal. His left hand was awkward with the utensil, but he managed to get most of a spoon up to his mouth, dropping the excess back into the bowl. He glanced back up to Ally, his eyes going wide.

"What are—"

Ally grabbed Max's arm and yanked it backwards for a better look. Max fell back with a yelp but Ally did not let go.

"Bullshit!" Ally said, smiling. "It's you!"

"Can you let me go?" Max asked. "You're twisting my arm."

"What is with you today?" Ted demanded. "You're going to make him run off. Again!"

"No, look!" she said, shoving Max's arm at Ted. "There's nothing there!"

"Okay," Ted said, removing Max's arm from Ally's hand. Max took back his arm and cradled his shoulder, Ted looking back to Ally like she'd gone crazy. "It's kinda dirty, but there's nothing there."

"No, you don't get it. There was, like, a second or third degree burn there yesterday. It was disgusting. And Harrison! I've been trying to figure out why half the cuts on his face are gone. I don't think he should even be conscious yet. But it's Max. It has to be. He's a healer."

"Seriously?" Ted looked Max over, his face splitting into a broad smile. "Dude awesome! We got a white mage! And I thought it was good enough that we finally got someone who actually knew first aid."

"We're never going to have to kidnap a doctor again. God, do you remember when we had to do that?" Ally asked Harrison. "That was you being a dumbass too."

Max stayed very still, hoping that they might not notice him sitting there. He didn't need this right now. He probably needed to make sure Harrison wasn't hurt permanently from his stupid actions last night and then he needed to get home where none of this was happening. Maybe he should sleep a bit in the middle somewhere.

He did not need to have Ally and Ted sounding quite so happy that he was one of them. He didn't even know how he was doing any of it — if he was doing it at all! Didn't they say they could do more things when more people showed up? Maybe it was someone else doing it.

Except you know that it's you doing it, he told himself. It explained how he managed to spill acid on himself and he ended up fine a couple hours later. He knew Harrison shouldn't be awake. He knew Jaime's bandages weren't that loose when he did them earlier.

He wasn't listening to anyone in the room, looking blankly forward at Jaime's ankle. Jaime was looking at him too and managed to catch his eyes. She put a finger up to her lips, telling Max to stay quiet.

"Guys," Harrison said, interrupting Ally and Ted. "I think you scared off your new healer."

Ally and Ted looked around, their eyes looking right at Max and continuing on to the rest of the room. Ally got up, looking around. "He better not be trying to leave again. We're not going to be able to save him this time. Come on, Ted, he can't have gotten far."

The pair of them left the room, Max sitting on the other side of the coffee table and letting it happen. Harrison watched them go before attempting to eat his oatmeal again, now cold. Jaime relaxed back in the couch and started to channel surf, the static on the television even lighter. "You're welcome."

"For wh— Oh!" Harrison said, dropping his spoon as soon as he saw Max. "Shit, I thought you were gone. Hey, are you okay?"

"I should fix that," he said, looking back at Jaime's ankle. He reached across the table and Jaime moved her leg closer to him, letting him unwrap the bandages. Underneath them, the marble of colours was now a dull red. "You should probably get more ice to keep the swelling down. I can get Ted—"

"You are not getting Ted," Harrison told him. "She'll survive without ice."

"It's better if she has some for the swelling."

"You're freaking out," Harrison told him, speaking slowly and looking at him intently. Max turned to look at him, finding himself staring back into Harrison's calm grey eyes. "Deep breaths, okay?"

Harrison started breathing long, slow breaths and Max found himself following along. It was stupid, but he started to calm down. Nothing about anything that happened here was making any sense and he somehow developed super powers without any real reason and, though that sense of panic would not stop, he could almost hear his own thoughts again.

"Better?" Harrison asked.

"No," Max told him. He turned back to Jaime's ankle and wrapped it again. "I don't know where we are. I don't know how we got here. I don't know what's happening to me or how I'm even doing any of this."

"It's a one day at a time thing," Harrison told him. "You'll start to get used to it until it finally just becomes normal."

"When does it start making sense?"

"It... doesn't. Ever. This stuff makes no sense, no matter what Ted says. You just kind of get used to it. Just try not to think too much about it and you'll get the hang of it pretty quickly."

"I should change the stuff on your arm," Max said, getting up and getting supplies out of the kit. He hoped this house had some more stuff to work with, because he was pretty sure he would be out of everything burn related after this. "How's it feeling?"

"Sore," Harrison said. "And it stings a little when I move it."

Max went to work slowly cutting and peeling the bandages off of Harrison's arm and wiping the areas he could clean to see how they were actually doing. Most of his bicep looked perfectly fine, if a bit pink. From the elbow down, he was still pretty bad but nowhere near as bad as last night. The charred skin was gone, replaced by fresh skin stretched thin and still blistering. He was careful not to pop any of them as he worked, but if Harrison moved too much, they would burst.

Harrison didn't look, keeping his eyes firmly on the television as Jaime switched between channels. Max was as gentle as he could manage, though he could feel every wince and hear every stifled groan that Harrison made as he worked to wrap his arm in clean bandages.

No one said anything as Max worked or even when he finished. He was getting low on materials to work with. He wouldn't be able to do this again. He didn't have the gauze or the sterile pads left to work with. He needed to check this house to see if there was anything he could use.

Harrison's eyes were back on him, thinking. "You just need a bit of space," he said at last. "Jaime, can you talk to Ally? Get her to back off for a bit?"

Jaime shrugged. Harrison seemed to take it as a yes. At Max's confused look, he said, "Ally's Jaime's cousin. Weird, right? I never would've guessed."

Max looked Jaime over. "You look nothing alike," Max said.

"And you look like crap," Jaime said, not looking at him. She switched to a news broadcast talking about a gang fight, then quickly to a court show.

"She's half," Harrison offered. "You do look a bit rough, though. Have you slept?"

"A little."

"Lie down," Harrison said, moving over on the couch to give him room.

"I'll be fine," Max said, though he could already feel himself nodding off. Whatever help breakfast had been, that energy had already drained out of him. He sat back against the couch and tried to stay awake, watching television through the light layer of static, but he was fighting a losing battle. It was back on the news, but not even a story about a fat cat being rescued was enough to help keep him awake.

Harrison didn't take notice of him, looking between the screen and Jaime. "How do you even know that remote's working?" he asked. "It's all just snow."

CHAPTER NINE

MAX WOKE UP curled up on the couch with a blanket over him. He felt light headed, but better than he had since this whole thing started. There was a soft hum running through his mind, soothing away much of the stress from the last couple days.

Light streamed in from behind the blinds as he sat up. Both Harrison and Jaime were gone, leaving him alone to stare at the television, now off. The slight scent of vomit still lingered in the couch cushions.

At least he was still in the same house.

Max got off the couch, stretching and grabbing his hoodie. It was cold and, even though it still smelled like burnt cotton, it was all he had for the moment. He needed a shower and a change, but his backpack was gone. It was still at the bus stop from the last time he left. Maybe he could find something that didn't smell like fire and sweat somewhere in the house.

He could hear something upstairs as soon as he left the room and he hoped that it was someone he knew up there. "Hey?" he called up the stairs. If it was them, then he had nothing to worry about. If it was a family of four waiting for him, at least they wouldn't completely freak out when they saw him. "You guys up there?"

The chattering quieted and Max slowed down as he went through the dining room into the kitchen. Ted was cutting up fruit and throwing it into a blender while Ally, Harrison and Jaime were sitting on the other side of the island watching him. Harrison's left his arm rested on the table, still bandaged but not nearly as red as before. Max should change that again.

"Hey," Harrison said. "You look better."

"I need a shower," Max said. "How's your arm?"

"Better every day. Looks like Jaime's completely back to normal, too."

"Good." Max took a seat at the bar, watching Ted cut up strawberries with everyone else. At least they were fine. He didn't really want to think about what was going on beyond that just yet. "Anything to eat?"

Ally got up and took a plate out of the fridge. "We saved a bit from last night," she said, throwing it in the microwave. "We weren't sure how long you were going to sleep for."

"Too long, sounds like," Max said. The microwave buzzed and Ally set the plate in front of him. Max didn't care what was on it and started in on the pasta, feeling a little better with every bite. "So where's Luke and Willow?" he asked between mouthfuls.

"They're holed up upstairs," Ted told him, the last of the fruit cut up and in the blender. "Luke's hurt or something. It happens sometimes. Usually they just lock themselves away until he gets better and then we're off on the never ending house tour again."

"But you know first aid, right?" Ally chimed in. He couldn't see the look Harrison gave her when she spoke, but she shrank away from it. "I mean, if you're feeling up to it, maybe you could check in on them and see if you can help him out?"

Max didn't even slow down as he worked through the last half of the plate. "Sure," he said between bites. "You're running out of bandages, though. Someone's going to have to fix that."

Ted turned on the blender, the machine whirring much more quietly than Max expected as it blended the fruit inside into a pulp. He added powder to it and a few more things and continued to blend until it was a very fine, thick puree. When he stopped and poured it into two glasses, there were still clumps that he tried to mix out with a fork. If Max wasn't already finished eating, he might have lost his appetite.

"We'll do a run later," Ally said. "I'm going to head up there in a bit if you want to come with."

She handed Max a glass and took the other, pulling him along to another set of stairs leading up before anyone could protest.

"You're in a hurry," he said. "What is this stuff?"

"It's for Luke and Willow," she explained. "They don't really eat anything that isn't in milkshake form."

"So what's the hurry?"

"No hurry," Ally said, She knocked on the door at the top of the stairs.

Willow was at the door, looking worse for wear. Her black hair was down and there were dark circles under her eyes, standing out in stark contrast to her pale skin. She took the glass from Ally and glared at her, then at Max.

"Max can help," Ally said, her hands moving and fingers dancing through the air as she talked. "He's a healer."

Willow looked Max over, a scowl on her face. Max felt something grab him and pull him forward past Ally and into the room. The door shut behind him, leaving Ally outside and him standing over the threshold of the doorway with a glass of smoothie in hand.

Against one wall of the large top floor room was a bed with Luke propped up in it, bandages arranged haphazardly around him. He could tell from here that whoever had done it barely knew how to put on a band-aid. The mix of tensor bandages and gauze without sterile pads underneath them and the spots of red leaking through told him that much.

As he got closer he noticed the light burns on his face and the laboured breathing. Stranger still was the complete lack of bandaging on his bare arms. Though Max could clearly see tears in his skin, there was no bleeding or scabbing on them at all. There didn't even appear to be any scarring. It looked like damage and he couldn't understand.

He got close enough to hand him the smoothie and Luke took it, trying and failing to cough. He saw the bandages around Luke's bruised ribs and reached over to touch them. Willow grabbed him by the arm and pulled him back.

"Sorry," Max said quickly. The image of Willow ripping a bus stop out of the concrete came to mind and he was not about to do anything to make her angry.

Luke shot her a look and she backed off, taking her smoothie and drinking it in the corner. Max could feel her eyes on him, but Luke looked at him apologetically and tried to smile. The smile turned quickly into a cough that wouldn't quite leave his throat.

The memory of Luke kidnapping him was back in his mind again. Looking at him now, Max couldn't bring himself to fear him. He was so pale and could barely breathe under those bruised and tightly bandaged ribs. He was too injured and weak to be threatening.

Max leaned over and gently started to remove the bandages, noting that no one had bothered to clean the concrete out of the scrapes before they wrapped him up. Many of the cuts were still open and had black bits sticking out of them. Some were starting to turn an uncomfortable shade of brown. "You're having trouble breathing, right?" he asked. "You're not supposed to wrap your ribs if you can help it. It keeps you from breathing properly."

Luke leaned forward at his insistence and Max got a better look at his arms as he unwrapped the bandages from his ribs. They were connected past the shoulder, the line between his skin and what had to be a prosthetic visible on his bicep. It was covered in what looked like skin, but through the tears, Max could only see darkness underneath.

"What happened?" he asked.

Luke started to move his hands, but Max couldn't understand what their movements meant.

"Sorry, I don't..." Max started, but he shook his head before he could finish. "Can you write?"

Luke tried moving his hand into the shape it would be if there actually were a pen in his hand and tried to move his wrist. The movement was jerky and he looked down at his hand and shook his head. Nope, a pen wasn't going to be much help.

"What about Willow?" he asked, already preparing for Willow to grab him again. "Ally tried teaching both of you, right?"

Luke rolled his eyes, looking flatly at Max. His hands came up, pointing at her and then his wrists flicked alternately. He signed something that looked like sign language again alternating with miming with his hands from the wrists down, Max getting the gist of it. Willow kept running off. Impatient. Didn't think it was worth it.

At least he knew Luke was willing to be friendly and might be up for a chat. When they got through the language barrier, Max might finally be able to get a few answers out of him. Once Max managed to put his confusion into the form of questions.

"I think your ribs are broken," Max said, looking at the marble of bruising on his chest. He pushed gently down on his sternum, Luke wincing against the pressure. Willow was out of her seat a moment later and at Max's side, grabbing his hand and pulling him back.

"Sorry!" he said. "I just needed to check. And he's going to need some painkillers to help with the pain."

Luke gave her a stern look and moved his arms at her. She let go of Max, but did not go back to her corner, instead gesturing back at him in a way similar to how Ally was moving her hands earlier. Max rubbed at his wrist as he watched, backing away to the door. While Luke seemed harmless enough, Willow was still a little too dangerous for his liking.

Willow turned back on him and grabbed him roughly by the arm.

A moment later, it was a lot noisier. There was soft music and a cool breeze drifting along the long halls and people wandering around. In front of him were vitamins organized by letter. He looked around to see the pharmacy department, though he couldn't see a store sign. Next to him, Willow made a gesture, telling him to hurry up.

"Okay," he muttered, walking through the aisles for something in a painkiller. There was a section, but nothing looked like it would be quite strong enough for what Luke was dealing with. Over the counter extra strength probably wouldn't cut it.

He looked up at the counter where three pharmacists were helping customers. Behind them were rows of small empty bottles and pills locked away. "It would be better if we could get some Tylenol 3," Max said to Willow.

Willow glared at him for a moment before vanishing. Max let out a breath he didn't know he was holding. He was forgetting something here, something important, but he couldn't quite remember what it was. There was also that soft sense of someone looking for him tugging at the back of his mind, faint but alarmingly present.

A phone beeped in the next aisle and his hand went to his pocket. Inside, he felt the pill bottle, the only thing he still had left from home. He hadn't taken any of his Adderall in a while and he probably needed it if he was going to keep himself together. He took one dry and went back to looking through the medical supplies.

Gauze, sterile pads and several other small things were in his hands when Willow returned with a small pill bottle of Tylenol 3 and a Russian name he couldn't pronounce on the label. She handed it to him, putting it on top of his handful of things and took his arm again.

"Do you have any... cash..."

They were back in the bedroom a moment later. Willow took the pill bottle off the top of Max's pile and pushed past him, removing the lid. She crushed one pill between her fingers into Luke's smoothie. Luke finished it off, a sour look crossing his face at the taste. Willow was gentle with him, smiling and removing the cup from his hands.

"Um, I'll let you finish up here," Max said, backing up to the door. "You're going to need to clean up the cuts and stuff, but you should really probably just rest until they fix themselves."

Willow didn't stop him as he made his exit. With supplies still in hand, he went back downstairs into the kitchen and set them down on the counter. Harrison still sat there, watching as Ted was still at work mixing something in a bowl with the water running in the sink over the blender.

"Go shopping?" Ted asked.

"Or something," Max said, his eyes falling on Harrison's bandaged arm. "I should change that before I forget."

"Hey Ally!" Ted called. "You don't need to get the stuff!"

"What stuff?" Ally called back from somewhere else in the

house. Max heard the footsteps come up the stairs and Ally appeared in the door. "Oh hey," she said to Max. "How'd it go up there?"

"Weird," Max said. He stripped the bandaged off of Harrison's arm and threw them out.

"Dude, that's gross," Ted said, grimacing and looking away from it.

Max looked it over again and didn't think it was that bad. A few nights ago it was nearly to his shoulder and looked like he was melting. Now, there was a definite arm there and the burns started just below the elbow. He didn't even have any scarring left behind from what had healed already, that skin still fresh and pink.

"I try not to look at it," Harrison told him. "At least it doesn't hurt that much anymore."

"It still looks well done enough to eat."

"That is disgusting, Ted," Ally said, coming over and getting a better look as Max started to bandage it back up again. "We'd need to at least season it a bit first."

"I worry about you sometimes," Harrison said, a smile on his face.

"Sorry Willow didn't let me in, Max," Ally said. "At least you got some supplies out of it. We weren't even sure what we needed."

Max was about to ask who she was referring to, but followed her waving hand to the door. Jaime leaned in the doorway, arms crossed and watching. She put most of her weight on her right, the ankle no longer seeming to bother her. Jaime gave him a little nod in thanks, but said nothing.

"Not that I could have been much help," Ally continued. "It's not like they've learned anything I've tried to teach them."

"I don't know how much of that stuff Luke could even do if he wanted to," Max said. He finished with the gauze on Harrison's arm and put what remained back in the box.

"Why not?"

"Because his arms are prosthetic?"

"No they aren't."

Max looked at her, then to the rest of them, trying to figure out if this was a joke. They seemed genuinely confused. "From about here down," he said, indicating the point he'd seen Luke's arm join his shoulder. "You seriously didn't know?"

"It's not like he goes sleeveless or takes his shirt off very much," Ally said.

"Ally would know." Harrison smirked at her.

Ally glared at him and Harrison backed down, though the smile did not leave his face. "We're going to pick up some stuff. We'll be back."

Ally left, grabbing Jaime to come with her on her way out.

They heard the two of them leave through the front door a moment later.

Max turned back to Ted and Harrison. They settled back into silence, watching as Ted took up the bowl and whisk again to continue making whatever batter he was working on. "So do you do anything else all day besides cook?" he asked.

"Not really," Ted said. He continued to whisk for a moment before he spoke again. "So they're really fake? I told you, Harrison, they're terminators or something."

CHAPTER TEN

MAX THREW HIS burnt hoodie back on and slipped out into the cool, quiet night after everyone had already fallen asleep. He was feeling better after a shower and new clothes brought back by Ally and Jaime, but a little restless. After spending the afternoon feeling a little drained, he wanted to go for a walk and see just where he'd ended up. His mind was buzzing with thoughts that wouldn't quite come together and he could use the fresh air.

He thought about home. He missed meeting up with Ashley to help her with Math. Jeremy was still probably freaking out. Tara was probably worried, too, and he'd missed classes. He wasn't even sure what day it was, but he wondered if they'd let him pass his classes anyway due to extenuating circumstances. He had been kidnapped, after all, and he wasn't even sure where he was.

He was aware that he could run right now. He could try to find a bus or flag down a car somewhere in these suburbs. He could knock on one of these doors and ask them to help him. Somehow, though, he found himself not seeing the point in it. He could go home, but why? There was nothing there for him but his friends. He could find new ones. He already had. And staying here meant he wouldn't have to worry about school or the police looking for him.

Max knew his thinking on that was off, but he couldn't quite place why.

He heard Harrison fall in step beside him before he saw him. Max didn't speed up or stop, continuing his steady pace and Harrison made no move to stop him. "Hey."

"Buddy system," Harrison said. "We aren't supposed to go out wandering all on our own in case last time happens again. And if I remember right, you would have been screwed without me there."

"I was kind of screwed with you there," Max reminded him. "Thanks, though."

"No problem. Look, we should get a bit farther from the house. You know, just in case."

Max didn't know in case of what, but he took the hand offered and let Harrison take him farther. They stopped walking and were in a different neighbourhood of much older houses that looked nothing like the neighbourhood they just left. It was colder and a little cloudier wherever they were, but there was a nice break from the rows of identical houses. Max dropped Harrison's hand, looking around.

"Where are we?" he asked, starting to walk again.

Harrison stayed beside him. "A couple neighbourhoods back," he said.

"Seems nice," Max said. "Where is this, exactly?"

"A little town called Mackenzie Falls," he said a wistful look in his eyes as he steered them into a park. "The house was just a couple blocks away from here."

"How do they keep finding these places?" Max asked, one of the hundreds of questions spinning around in his head finally coming together. "I mean, are they always these big houses? Where do they even find them? They all seem like there should be people living in them."

"They're on vacation," Harrison told him. "Somehow, Luke and Willow always seem to find these huge houses of people who are away on vacation for a while and we kind of just... live there in the mean time. Just until they find the next place and everyone's ready to get moving again. Or until they find us again. Then we usually just book it out of there to the next place."

"So we're just moving from house to house hoping no one comes back early from vacation and no one finds out that we're squatting *and* hoping that we aren't found by the men in black?"

"You get used to it," Harrison said with a shrug. "After four or five houses, you stop getting that attached to the locations and you just kind of, I don't know, deal with it. Luke and Willow know what they're doing."

"What do you even know about them?" Max asked.

Harrison was quiet for a long moment "Not much," he said, seeming a little uncomfortable. "They don't really talk much, you know? We were kind of like their cats at first, I guess. They'd move and we'd go with them. They'd try to make sure there was enough space. When we didn't have enough food, Jaime and I worked out a system to get more."

Max didn't say anything when Harrison stopped. He looked around, finding a swingset and wandered towards it, Harrison keeping in step beside him.

"After Jack and Mary, Luke and Willow started leaving a lot more often. Willow got real nervous about people leaving for a while and the grocery runs were out. Then they found Ted. Well, Luke found him. Luke finds everyone. Willow just goes off and comes back without bringing anything or anyone back. Well, maybe injuries. I know she's come back injured before. Not as bad as Luke, though. Just a scratch or two maybe."

"Who are Jack and Mary?"

"Who?" Harrison asked.

"You just said something about Jack and Mary," Max said.

Harrison wasn't listening to him anymore. He took a seat in one of the swings and started to rock back and forth in it.

Max frowned but sat next to him. Maybe he just didn't want to talk about them. That was fine. He could ask about them later. There were more questions.

"So what are we doing here?" Max asked. He started to swing and Harrison matched him. "Are they actually taking us somewhere or are we just wandering around, picking up more and more people before the white woman or the lady in white or whatever catches us? We're not just running, are we?"

Harrison let out a bit of a laugh. "I've been trying to figure that out," Harrison admitted. "Ally's got a map on her. We're keeping track of where the houses all are and trying to figure out where we're actually heading. We are going in a direction and it looks like there's somewhere they're taking us, but it's a bit tough trying to figure it out."

"Oh," Max said. That was comforting, at least. "And?"

"Canada."

"What?"

"Maybe Vancouver-ish?" Harrison said, using his body to swing even higher. "That's what it looks like, anyway. I think. Even though all the houses seem to be kind of scattered and some of them backtrack a little, we seem to be heading right to the border."

"Backtracking?"

"The place we're in now? It's on the other side of the same town we were in before you. We went backwards again. We're in Oregon now. Still. We're slowly getting somewhere, though. They seem to be conspiring more than before. Luke and Willow, I mean. I think we're getting close to wherever it is they want to be. We've been moving a lot faster, anyway. Really, Ally needs to hurry up with the sign language thing so we can actually ask them stuff."

Max couldn't argue with that. He couldn't really argue with much while he was on the swing. The wind whipping by his ears as he rose and fell, going back and forth, was too relaxing. He wanted nothing more than to let this continue for a little while. It was peaceful at night and he didn't really want to think about any of this stuff anymore.

"So," he said. "Where is everyone originally from?"

"I'm Florida," he said. "I think Jaime was Jersey. They found Ally in Georgia and we picked up Ted going through California."

"Florida?"

Harrison laughed. "I'm not as crazy as the Florida stories. We all have to come from somewhere and we haven't even left your state yet. It's actually nice here."

"Thanks," he said. "You get used to it. You said Mackenzie Falls? We probably shouldn't be out. If you're right about the wanted thing, the cops are probably looking for me. In the middle of the night. Swinging on a swing set. In the middle of a city near the border. We're almost in Nevada, aren't we?"

Max wasn't sure why, but he felt calmer than he had in months. He was probably a wanted man and possibly considered on the run. He didn't have a home to go back to. He was travelling with a bunch of people who had also been kidnapped and thrown into a comic book universe where super powers existed. Not to mention, he was out in the open where he could easily be caught by the police if they came by. His lack of panic over any of this bothered him as much as his lack of desire to run.

"So, before all this," Harrison said, breaking him out of his reverie, "what were you doing? School? Friends? Girlfriend? Video games?"

Max shrugged. "Yeah, the usual I guess. Did okay in school. I wasn't failing anything, anyway. Friends, family, games. I dunno, pretty normal, I guess except for the job thing. I was training to be a lifeguard. Most of my friends were just going to go off and camp for most of the summer, but I'm hoping for a car next year and my parents aren't buying it for me."

"Don't bother," Harrison told him. "If your parents aren't paying for the car, they probably won't pay for the gas either and that stuff is *expensive*."

Max shrugged. "They might. And if not, I might still be able to afford gas if I keep lifeguarding for a while. What about you? What were you doing before all of this started for you?"

Harrison hesitated. "School, home. Had to watch my little sister sometimes. Had a friend who had a car, though. He drove me around to do stuff on the weekends, but we kind of had a falling out just before all this happened. I kind of miss it, you know?"

Max shrugged. "I don't know," he said. "It's a nice change not having to worry about homework anymore. No tests, no pop quizzes, no corrosive acid. I kind of miss my friends, though."

"But no girlfriend?"

Max shrugged, feeling uncomfortable again. "I'm just not interested in dating right now," he said, the line as rehearsed now as it was when he told Tara just a couple of days ago. If it was a couple days. It felt like a whole lifetime now.

"Not interested?" Harrison's tone became very curious at that. "What does that—"

"We have to get out of here," Max said suddenly, his feet lowering to the ground and he tried to bring his swing to a stop. He could feel it again, like someone was there and looking for him.

Unlike last time, he was going to get them out of there before something happened. Harrison would listen. He might have to talk quickly, but Max would make him understand that they had to get out of here now.

Harrison looked back down at him, confused. He stopped

actively kicking, letting the swing's momentum carry him, but made no effort to slow down. "Why?" he asked, looking genuinely worried.

"Someone's coming," Max said. "One of the guys in the suits. We have to get out of here right—"

The world went sideways and his body flew to one side at the bars holding the swings. He flailed through the air, trying not to hit the support beams. His leg caught against it, a very distinct snap echoing painfully through his body as his knee popped out of the socket, followed by a sickening crack that echoed throughout the small park. His body kept going and his back ran into another beam, his ears ringing loudly as his head collided with metal.

Max dropped to the ground, very certain that the howl of pain that filled the air was his own.

Through his blinding pain, he saw Harrison collapsing on the grass on the other side of the swings. Both hands clutched his head and he curled up into himself. Harrison took one hand carefully off his head and put it on the ground, slowly trying to push himself up.

He caught Max's eye, just as a familiar woman in white showed up between the two of them. She looked over to Max. There were no glasses on her, instead her eyes looking very red and her face sympathetic. She paused, looking between them, hesitating before turning toward Max.

She looked so strange. The white suit he thought of her in was there, but there was also a long skirt at the same time. The glasses were there, so thick he couldn't see her eyes, as well as her bare face with red eyes looking down at him. He felt like he wasn't seeing any of it properly — like they weren't really there. She moved her hands in a manner he'd seen before. A fist rubbing small circles on her chest. It was like she was trying to say she was sorry.

His eyes drifted past her to Harrison. He got to his feet slowly, wavering back and forth, holding his bandaged arm close to himself.

The woman now looked like she should, dressed in the suit and sunglasses. She was looking around at the neighbourhood, a little confused at how she had managed to get here. She looked back at Harrison, impressed even though he was stumbling back and forth.

She turned back to Max, but Max wasn't watching her. Behind her, Harrison stopped, and there was a flash of a familiar goth girl, appearing behind him as he stumbled again. She caught him and she vanished, taking Harrison with her.

The woman in white looked behind her and saw that Harrison was no longer there.

Max felt the presence of someone behind him and soon he was no longer there either.

Max was back inside a moment later, though he did not

notice if it was the same house. Willow brought him here standing upright and the pain in his leg sent a shockwave through his body. He fell back to the ground, unable to keep from letting out a scream of pain. He thought his knee was dislocated. Did dislocation really hurt this much?

He looked down at his leg and saw the jagged white of his bone piercing through his blood soaked jeans. There was nothing after that.

CHAPTER ELEVEN

MAX WOKE TO a sharp pain shooting through his leg. His eyes flew open and he let out a hiss through his teeth as the pain subsided. It settled into the same ache that engulfed the rest of his body. He knew if he stayed still, at the very least the pain would not increase. His head spun, but he tried to figure out just where he was.

It was a very pretty, pink room, if uncomfortably warm. It was fit for a princess which, given how dizzy he was, he might just be right now. There were fairies painted on the wall and a nice mural of a magical garden on one side of the room. There was even a doll house in the shape of a castle, with a princess in the tower and a prince lying on the ground.

Max could use a prince right about now. One with some amazing painkillers.

His eyes continued down until he saw his leg. He immediately looked away, the white of his bone still sticking out of his jean leg. The blood was dry now and he could see that someone had put plastic under him to keep him from bleeding through the bed.

Dreams of a prince coming for him evaporated as he remembered what happened. The playground. The woman in white. Slamming into the metal bars of the swing set.

His back and left shoulder were badly bruised. The welt on the back of his head still stung against the plastic covered pillow. His kneecap was knocked out of place. Below that...

Max winced with the effort it took to sit and bit back a yelp of pain. Every movement sent a sharp stab of pain through every nerve in his body and a fresh wave of dizziness threatened to knock him back, but he needed to get a better look at his leg.

He felt nauseous knowing that it was his bone sticking up, but his jeans, now caked in dried brown blood, hid most of the injury from his eyes. He knew it wasn't pretty under there and that his body had only just gotten the two pieces of bone close enough together to start stitching them. He'd heal a lot faster if he could just get the two pieces in line with one another.

His left arm hurt too much to move, so he reached down with his right. One quick push. He could do this.

This time, Max knew it was his scream that pierced the air.

MAX WOKE UP still lying on plastic in the pink room. It was dark now and he was in no less pain than before. He didn't know how he managed to sleep.

He struggled a second time to sit up, this time a little easier than the last. His leg was still there, the bone at slightly less of an angle. Even in the darkness, he could tell there was fresh blood around the bone and on his hand. With better contact, his body was repairing the bone much more quickly. It had worked, though he wasn't done yet.

"Okay," he muttered to himself. "Just a little more. You can do this."

He took a deep breath and brought his hand back over the bone. He let it hover there, waiting for a wave of dizziness pass. Just a little more and his body could take over from there.

"No!" someone called in the darkness. "Harrison!"

Jaime grabbed him by the shoulders and forced him back down. Max's cry of surprise turned to one of pain as his leg twitched from the movement. His shoulder slammed back into the bed and he recoiled against Jaime. Jaime struggled to keep him down, but a third hand appeared to help.

Max could feel the tears in his eyes as the pain shot through his body. He couldn't catch his breath, panting and whimpering. He tried to move, to clutch his leg, to curl into his shoulder, to do anything that would make it hurt less, but the hands would not let him move.

"It's okay," he heard in soft whispers around him. "It's going to be okay. Just breathe. Come on. It's going to be okay."

The steady sound of deep breathing. Slowly, he managed to match those breaths and he relaxed. The stabbing pains stopped when he did. The breathing burned his throat, but he kept at it until the hands finally loosened their grip.

"God, you are a dumbass," Jaime said. She turned on the fairy covered lamp on the bedside table.

Max winced against the light, letting out a fresh groan of pain. He was dizzy from the effort and he couldn't see anything through the tears in his eyes. His body was made of pain and exposed nerve endings. Worse, that bone was still sticking out.

"What were you trying to do?" Harrison asked, finally taking his hand off of Max's shoulder.

"It needs to be straight," he said. His voice came out as a hoarse whisper. "It's not going to heal sticking out. Let me just—"

Harrison and Jaime both pushed him back down to the bed. "You're running a fever, Max," Harrison told him. "You need to rest."

"It's almost there."

"No."

"Water first," Jaime said, looking to Harrison. The weight of Harrison's hand disappeared along with the rest of him and Jaime gave Max a long look. He opened his mouth to speak when the door opened in front of him, Ally dressed in a large shirt looking in and turning the light on.

"Everything okay?" she asked, rubbing her eyes. "I thought I heard screaming."

"All him," Jaime said. "You were right."

Ally looked more concerned than annoyed as she came closer to the bed. Her eyes went to his leg, frowning and then back to Max.

Harrison came back a moment later with a glass of water in hand, passing it to Max. He took it in his good hand, looking at it and trying to figure out how he was supposed to drink it without spilling it all over himself. He let it rest on his chest and Ally rolled her eyes at Harrison. "I think I saw a bunch of straws in the third drawer from the dishwasher," she said.

Harrison was gone again, then back a moment later with one. Ally helped Max sit and put the straw in his glass. Max forgot just how much he loved water until that moment, the cool liquid like rain to the desert that was his throat. Drinking left him dizzy and Ally pulled the glass away, forcing him to take a breath before he continued.

"You should eat something," Ally said. "And we're going to need to get your pants off."

"What?" Harrison asked.

"Now that he's conscious, we should probably fix his leg. You know, before he eats something he's just going to throw up all over the place when we try to fix it."

"Shouldn't he eat something so he has something to throw up?" Jaime asked.

"Here, I'll get them off." Ally took out a pair of scissors.

"Why are you just carrying scissors?" Harrison demanded.

"Max," Ally said, removing the glass from Max's hand and placing it on the bedside table, "are you still with us?"

Max groaned in agreement as another wave of nausea swept over him. He missed the water already.

"What do we need to do with your leg to help you?"

Max blinked at her. Leg. She was asking about his leg.

"Max stay with me. What do I need to do?"

"Make it straight," he muttered. "It needs to be straight."

"Okay," Ally said. "You guys might want to hang on to him."

Max watched dully as Ally got to work, cutting his pant leg off. She cut and peeled it away in strips, Max flinching when the material came away with hair and skin still attached to it. She worked as slowly and as carefully as she could to keep from hurting him too badly, but there wasn't much she could do.

When she was done, she hesitated and looked back around the room. She went to the toy castle and held a Ken doll in front of Max's mouth. "Bite this," she said.

"What are you doing?" Harrison asked.

"I see it in the movies," Ally said. "There has to be a reason they do it."

Max let her put the doll in his mouth and watched as Ally went back to his leg. She looked at the bone and went a little green at the sight of it, her lips tightening into a line and the lump in her throat settling back down. She refused to look away from it and took another deep breath.

"This is such a bad idea," Harrison muttered.

"Push it in, then we find a way to splint it, right?" Ally asked. She didn't look at any of them as she talked. "I can do this. Just one little push. Just one little—"

Max wasn't ready for it when Ally pushed down. The bone cracked as she threw all her weight onto it, forcing it back into place. It was the worst pain he'd ever been in and far more than he could handle. He blacked out.

◆————◆————◆

THIS TIME, THE room was blue. It was smaller than the last one, with no princesses or fairies or castles or promises of princes to come save him, but it did have a television, two doors on the wall and the sound of someone softly snoring.

Max felt weak and sore all over. He was hungry and the room felt like it was on a particularly rocky boat, but it was much better than the last time he was awake. For one thing, he didn't feel like there was a bone sticking out of his leg. For another, though it hurt to try, he could move his left arm.

He pushed himself up to sit and get a better look around the room, the movement not causing nearly the amount of pain it had before. "Hello?" he said, his voice still hoarse. "Someone the — Ah!"

His leg shifted, the pain shooting up through his body. A fresh wave of dizziness gripped him and he inhaled in small, quick gasps. Though the rest of his body didn't feel nearly as bad this morning, his leg was nothing but pain with every movement.

He just needed to stop moving. Moving made it worse.

Ted shot up from one side of the bed, the snoring stopping. He glanced down at Max's leg before forcing himself to look at Max. "Awake?"

"Yeah," Max said tightly. "Pretty awake." His eyes went down to his leg which was still largely open, the layers of skin still too thin to hide the muscles stitching themselves together underneath. He could feel the bone getting to work fusing itself back together, but it was still not ready to put any weight on. Someone had fashioned a splint around it consisting of two pieces of wood wrapped together with medical tape at the top and bottom of his shin.

"Ally said it should get air or something," Ted said, carefully not looking at his leg.

"Knee's still dislocated," Max said, leaning forward. His leg resisted the motion, but he continued forward. "I should pop it back in."

"I don't think so," Ted said, gently pushing his arm back down. "We'll make Ally do that."

"You could do it."

"No. No I cannot. Ask me anything else."

Max hesitated. As the pain in his leg settled into a strong, pulsing ache, he realized there was something else he needed to do.

"Is the washroom nearby?" he asked, not meeting Ted's eyes.

Ted went stiff for a moment, then got to his feet and went to Max. "I'm not going in with you," he said, helping Max up. Max was in agony as Ted helped him out of bed and to one of the two doors on the wall. He let him into the small room consisting of nothing but a toilet and a sink.

It was an experience he never wanted to repeat, though he

knew he would have to. He barely managed and he got back to the door on his own where Ted helped him back to the bed. Once he was settled again, Ted handed him a plate of appetizers.

"So," Max said, placing it beside him and taking a sausage roll off of it. "What happened?"

"Well," Ted said, still carefully avoiding looking at Max's leg even when he looked away, "we moved again. Twice. Looks like every time you leave the house you seem to draw out the guys after us, so you're currently under house arrest."

"I have no idea how you guys plan on keeping me in here," Max said flatly, looking at his leg. He should wrap it up properly. He also needed to get his knee popped back into place, since it wasn't going to do that on its own. His super healing might kick in and do it, but it would be a lot faster if he did it himself.

He really might have super healing.

"Hey," Ted said. "You feeling okay?"

"My leg has a very large gaping wound in it and my knee is dislocated," Max told him. "And everything hurts. I'm just great."

"Yeah, it's kind of weird," Ted said, resisting the urge to look down. "We thought you'd just fix yourself up, but it's been a week."

"*A week?*"

"*Eat*," he insisted. "Look, we kind of need you to not die right about now. After we left the last place, Harrison's hand stopped getting any better and Luke's really not doing that good either. Ally thinks that it's got something to do with people only getting fixed if you're conscious."

"How do you figure?"

"Jaime said you pushed your bone back in place," he said. "When you did that, you started to get better. And then Ally said that you got her to get it the rest of the way and now you're looking a lot better. And eating. And shitting all on your own."

Max wasn't sure how to take that, finishing the meal and feeling a little better for it. His eyes went back to his leg, seeing the slow progress it was making and trying to determine how best to clean it out for himself when he knew how much it hurt to bend down to touch it. "I should bandage it properly."

"Yourself?"

"Well, no one's done it so far," Max pointed out. "Is there a first aid kit here somewhere?"

"Give me a minute," Ted said, leaving him alone in the room to think.

He wondered how long it would take to fix his leg with a gaping wound like that. He could almost feel his body working on stitching itself up, bit by bit mending his bones and trying to return his shoulder to its normal state. There might be a way to make it go faster, though he didn't know where he'd even start with that.

A week ago, Jeremy said he was Batman.

This all started on a Friday. What was after that? He woke up, but he wasn't sure how long he'd slept. Maybe just through the night and they'd been in the city. They left the city that evening when the men in black came after them. They were in a different house after that for two days. So it was three days that he was awake for that he'd been gone and about a week that he'd been unconscious for. It seemed longer than that, somehow, but he wasn't really sure how much longer. Or shorter. How long as a week, anyway? Seven days technically, but it could be less or more when other people talked about it.

There were people worried about him. Concerned. He'd been out a week and woken up only to start screaming as he tried to fix his bones with his bare hands. It was stupid and he didn't really know what he was doing. Just as bad that he'd made Ally fix the rest of it.

The alarm on the table beeped and his hand went to his pocket. He hadn't taken an Adderall in a while. He should do that.

His pocket was empty. Max checked his other one and turned it out, but both were empty. It must have fallen out while he was at the swings. The next little while until he got more was going to suck. If he could even get any replacement pills now that he was on the run and without his prescription.

"Max!"

He looked up to see Ally at his bedside next to Ted. She looked annoyed, but Ted ignored her, putting the familiar kit from the apartment on the bed.

"Sorry," he said.

"Look, Ted tells me you're planning on doing stupid stuff again and that's not going to happen."

"Huh?" he asked. "Right, he left to get the kit."

"Yeah," Ted said, looking uncomfortable. "And now he's going to leave because he doesn't want to see what's going to happen next."

"And you are going to walk me through whatever you're planning on doing to yourself," Ally told him. "We can't just have one person who knows how to work a first aid kit in this place. Okay?"

Max smiled. "Sure," he said, genuinely grateful that she was willing to help. "First thing I need you to do is pop my kneecap back into place."

They started on the lesson, Max trying not to react too much and Ally being much more rough than he was ready for. She was able to shove his knee back into place, though used the same aggression on cleaning and bandaging. Max was patient despite the pain and coaxed her into being a bit more gentle, encouraging as many breaks as he could so he could catch his breath and recover from the fresh waves of pain and nausea.

"So I'm under house arrest," he said when they were finally

finished. Ally found a few Tylenol to help, though they were not nearly strong enough.

"It's not like you can really leave right now anyway," Ally pointed out. "Did you want a book or something?"

A thought struck Max and he shook his head. "Do you know what this means?" he asked, balling his hand into a fist and rubbing it in a small circle on his chest. "Is it sign language or something?"

"Yeah," Ally said. "That's sorry. Where'd you pick that one up?"

"I saw it somewhere," Max said. "You think you can teach me more?"

CHAPTER TWELVE

ENTERTAINMENT WAS HARD to come by over the next few days. There was the daily beeping of that alarm at 9am, but the clock didn't even have radio on it. He found the remote, but there was no cable and no DVD player, not that he could get up to change the disks in it anyway. He was left trying to listen in on whatever was happening in the rest of the house, but his room was sound proof. Worse, they kept leaving his door closed and there was no air conditioning, leaving Max to try and endure the heat with no distractions.

At least he wasn't forgotten. Ally was a frequent visitor, as was Luke. Max walked Ally through how to deal with damaged ribs, what little he actually knew, and she taught them both sign language in exchange. When Ally wasn't there, Luke would still come by to practice with him.

Willow, as Luke managed to explain in jumbled sign language, didn't like Max that much right now. Max could hardly blame her, since this was the second time she had to save him.

Harrison did not visit, even with his injuries. Ally told him that she would take care of them, but he knew there was more to it than that. He could tell Harrison was avoiding him. He would linger just outside of his door sometimes, but never came in. It almost felt like something kept him from coming in, but he couldn't tell what.

Every morning, he would see Ted when he brought breakfast and he stuck around, hiding from doing dishes and claiming he was there to keep Max company. Max didn't mind, Ted doing his best to offer movie or television show examples of how he should try to make his healing stronger. Max doubted the visualization would work, but he didn't let Ted know. It was nice to give him an excuse to come visit and kill some of his boredom.

They pushed the bed next to the washroom door so he could use it without assistance and left him alone most of the day with a few books piled beside the bed. Max couldn't bring himself to focus on any of them long enough to get through them, instead letting himself drown in his own thoughts for hours until sleep took him. Though he tried to push the darker thoughts away, they kept creeping back in.

His life back home was gone now. He knew that much. He had been gone for weeks. He'd missed enough lifeguard training that he'd have to retake it at this point if he did ever get back. His friends would be in finals now and getting ready for their summer plans, Max forgotten about in the jumble of everything else happening in their own lives.

He didn't have a home to go back to, either. His parents were dead. He saw them, shot and lying in their own blood at the front door to the house. At this point, he'd missed the funeral because he was busy running around with a bunch of people he barely knew, getting beaten up by strangers with super powers. The same ones that shot his parents in his home because they were trying to protect him.

They're dead.

He covered his eyes in the darkness with his arm, unable to hold back the tears. At least he didn't say anything he regretted when he last saw them alive. It was a small comfort, but it did nothing to bring them back.

Even if he did make it back, Harrison warned him that he'd be wanted for murder. Ally warned him of the same thing.

He wanted to go home, but there was no home left for him to go back to.

Ally came by early on the fourth morning with new books for

the stack. "How's the leg?" she asked, taking a seat at his bedside and rummaging through the rest of the stack.

"Sore."

"You doing okay?"

Max shrugged with both shoulders, the pain almost gone from his upper body. "It hurts to stand. I don't think I can manage walking yet. Oh, and my parents are dead and I can never go home. I'm doing great."

Ally went quiet and got back to her feet. She went back to the door and gently closed it, before returning to his bedside. She opened her mouth to say something, but the words died on her lips. She was sympathetic, but looked away, unable to think of anything to say.

They sat in silence for a long while, Ally rubbing the back of her neck awkwardly before she made her next move. With a quick glance at the shut door, Ally turned back and leaned in close. "Harrison said you asked where Luke and Willow are taking us, right?"

It took Max a moment to remember. It seemed so long ago. "He also said something about someone named Jack and Mary."

"No idea who they are," Ally said, going to the wall and taking a map of the United States off of it. She spread it out across the empty side of his bed. "So this is what Harrison and I have seen so far. They found Jaime back in Jersey, though I have no idea how she got there."

"Isn't Jaime your cousin?" Max asked. "How do you not know?"

"Jaime went missing over a year before they found me. She won't tell me what happened. I thought she was a guy for a long time. Anyway, after we found Harrison, we stayed in an apartment for about two weeks. After that, we started moving about every week and took a bit of a long route along the bottom of the States. Whenever they ran into the suits, we would go back a little to throw them off, or take a turn up into somewhere else and once went down to Mexico. Up here is where we got Ted," she pointed out, their path taking a large turn backwards. "And then when we got you," she continued, pointing out the path and the sharp turn to pick him up. "And now we're about here."

Their path was moving slower back on the previous path up the west coast now, Ally pointing out the stops they made on the way to their current house.

"I don't think we're heading to Canada," Max offered.

"*Harrison* thinks its Canada," Ally said, a little annoyed. "Jaime too. Or she did before."

"Before what?"

"About Texas?" Ally considered it a moment before shaking her head. "I don't know. We used to talk a lot more before Texas. I think something happened. Now she just keeps heading off all day on her own. She knows she's not supposed to, but she's not even taking Harrison or me with her anymore. No idea what's up with her. Anyway, I'm pretty sure it's something in Washington. Whatever it is that we're going towards, we had better be almost there. It's been at least a year now."

"When did you start all of this?" he asked.

"May fourteenth."

"It's been over a year," he told her. When she looked at him, he replied, "It was May thirtieth when Luke got me."

She hesitated a moment before brushing it off. He got a flash of something, a man and woman coupled with a feeling of home and warmth and a great deal of sadness, before she went back to the map. "I'm pretty sure that we're heading to somewhere in Washington. We started moving a lot faster just before we got you. I think it's got something to do with us almost getting there."

Ally frowned. "You know, they've been a little weird lately. Well, Willow's always been a little distant, but Luke's never been this into trying to talk before. Usually when Willow decides she doesn't want to do it anymore, he just follows her out."

"He keeps coming in to talk, too," Max said. "I think he wants to talk about what's going on, but Willow doesn't want him to. And Willow apparently *really* doesn't like me so..."

"How do you figure?"

Max looked at the window. He knew this feeling. "Luke's coming."

"Luke's not in the house."

"Hide the map," he said. "Now."

Ally complied, snatching up the map and shoving it under the bed. She looked at Max strangely, but Max's eyes went to the corner where Luke appeared, looking much more cheerful now that his ribs were nearly mended. Ally followed his eyes and jumped, turning back to Max accusingly, but saying nothing.

Luke offered Ally a nod and turned to Max and moved his hands. His fingers were clumsy as he signed, not always moving as they tried to make the shapes, but Max had learned to read them without trouble. *Willow got hurt. She's being an idiot. Come help.*

"What do you expect me to do?" Max asked out loud. He didn't remember what any of the signs were to respond with. "I can't really move. Can she come here?"

He rolled his eyes. *Are you sure you can't get up for a little while?*

Max looked back at his leg, no longer bleeding under the bandages but now a marble of colours that no person should be. Mending a completely severed fibula, as it turned out, took much longer to heal than burned hands or crushed ribs. Though Max's patients were better, his healing was taking much longer than he expected. "I am definitely not getting up. If you want me to do anything, you're going to have to bring her here."

Luke rolled his eyes, clearly displeased, and disappeared from the room. Ally stared at him, Max shifting uncomfortably under her gaze. Finally, she leaned over and looked around before asking, "How did you do that?"

"Do what?" he asked.

"You knew he was coming!" she said.

Max shrugged. "Just a feeling."

"And what he was saying?"

Max looked at her, trying to decide if she was screwing with him. "He was using sign language," he said slowly. "You've been teaching both of us."

"What exactly did he say?"

Max knew she was expecting something out of him, but he didn't know what. "He said Willow was hurt," he said, watching Ally for her reaction. "He wanted me to go up and help her. I told him I couldn't do that. And then he left."

"And what does that look like?"

"You were right—"

"No. *Show me* what it looks like."

Max hesitated, looking at her. Her arms were crossed and waiting for him to make a move. He held up his hands and tried to remember what Luke did, but he couldn't remember anything about the movements besides them being clumsy.

"Ted!" Max said, turning to the closed door. "Right on time!"

Ted opened the door with a plate of pancakes.

"How did you know *he* was coming?"

"He comes by every morning," Max said. "Same time."

"Something's weird with you," Ally said, leaving the room. "I'll be back."

Ted watched her out, laughing a little and setting Max's breakfast down on the table for him. "Your game must be even worse than mine."

"What?" Max asked. "No! No, that's not it. No."

"She *is* cute."

Max let out an irritated groan and Ted smiled, letting it drop. "What was that about, then?" he asked.

"I don't know," he said. "Luke showed up and apparently Willow's been hurt, so he was asking if I could come up to take a look at her which, obviously not happening."

Ally came back in with the medical kit while he was talking, opening it and handing Max his morning painkillers. "And you understood it," she said, watching as Max took them dry before starting in on the pancakes.

"What?" he asked between bites.

"Max, you haven't learned that much," Ally pointed out. "You've only been doing this for a couple days."

"It's not that hard to pick up," Ted offered.

"It's not three days easy," Ally countered.

Max went over everything she'd tried to teach them over the last few days, but found himself coming up short. Now that he thought about it, all they really went over was vocabulary at this point. Luke would come in after and have full conversations despite how little they learned, but Max figured that the majority of those conversations were him being really good with charades to fill in the blanks.

Luke appeared with Willow before Max could think on it much more. Both Ted and Ally jumped at the sudden appearance, but Max could see why Luke wanted him to get a look at her. Luke held her by the arms with her back facing Max so he could see the deep gash starting from her shoulders and down to her other side. The back of her dress was torn and bloody from it as she struggled out of Luke's hands. Her movements were jerky and he could hear her intake of breath as she winced.

"Ow!" Ted winced at the sight of it. "How did you do that?"

"Um," Max said, panicking as he realized what this would mean. He would need to get a better look and he wasn't about to ask Willow to take her dress off so he could see it better. His eyes flew to Ally, wide and pleading with her to do something.

Ally smiled at him and waited. She was enjoying this a little too much. She made two gestures with her hands. *Later. Everything.*

Max nodded. Whatever she wanted.

"I'll patch you up," Ally said, a satisfied smile crossing her lips. "Max can do his thing after. Ted, out."

Ted left as Ally brought Willow over the bed to the washroom. Max winced as the bed shifted when they stepped on it, but managed to keep his leg mostly still. Luke took a seat on the bed, making Max's leg shift again, though he didn't seem to notice Max's pain. Instead, he looked at the door, frowning.

"What happened?" Max asked.

Checking out the next house, he said. *We're moving on again tomorrow, probably. We were, anyway.*

"Were?"

Well, it looks like they managed to find us again.

"You mean the guys in the suits?"

There was another place we looked at. It should be just as good, but we're not really sure when the family is coming back for that one. Leaving tomorrow at some point, so it might slow us down a bit. They're tracking us down faster, and we've been here for too long already. Covering you up is getting tiring, so we're going to have to start moving a lot more now.

"Wait, so I'm the reason they keep finding us?"

Luke hesitated, thinking over his hands first before continuing. *Willow thinks you're part of it. You are incredibly easy to track down if anyone's looking for you.*

"I'm what?"

I could tell where you were down to the high school from thousands of miles away. It took me a lot longer to find everyone else. You are like a beacon. The weird thing is, keeping you in a place with a bunch of people like us, it seems to hide you a lot better. You leave with just one other person and you start to be a beacon again. Granted, they'll only notice if they're looking for you, but you do have pretty terrible luck on that front.

"It doesn't look like I'm going anywhere any time soon," Max said, trying not to think of himself as a beacon for the people after them. "Why would they be tracking us down faster? Are we getting close to something?"

Looks like they're done.

Max turned back around to find Willow with a bandage across her back and holding the front of her dress in place with her hands. She was scowling deeper than Max had ever seen before and turned her back to Max. He could feel her impatience and desire to get out of the room.

He could feel that it was quite deep when he tentatively touched the bandage. He imagined it fixed, the skin healed over and everything sealed shut again. He traced his finger along the length of it, gentle and trying to ignore the other scars covering her back.

As soon as he reached the end, Willow rolled her shoulders back, a twitch of pain spreading across them. He pulled his hand back and the back of the dress fastened itself again. She turned back to shoot a glare at Luke, her mind on a house right on the border right before Washington and vanished from sight.

Luke rolled his eyes and looked apologetic before he left. *Be back.*

Ally looked at him, looking confused and disbelieving of what she saw. "Did he say where he was going?" she asked. She'd been smiling since Willow exited the washroom.

"To check out the next house we're heading off to."

"And what did the sign for that look like?"

Max opened his mouth to speak and then stopped. He raised his hands in front of him, but they could not quite remember what Luke had done. They twitched one way or another, trying to remember what his hands were doing at the time, and then what those signs actually looked like. He could remember what various weather was and walk and a few other things, but he was unable to come up with anything that would signify a house that he was almost certain was in Washington.

"Hey!" Ally snapped, eyes squeezed shut and rubbing at the back of her head. Max looked up, not sure how long he was trying to figure that out for. "I get it, you don't know. Did he say when he was going to be back?"

"Not really," Max told her.

"So what else were you guys talking about over there?"

"Well, he said he and Willow were looking for the next house and ran into the guys in the suits. Apparently we're getting close to something and I think that's why they keep showing up wherever we've been."

"And it's not you?"

"Nope," he said. It might be, but she didn't need to know that, especially given that look she was giving him now. He held her eyes until she was satisfied. She didn't look convinced, but she left him alone anyway. She knew that she'd get answers out of him eventually.

CHAPTER THIRTEEN

ALLY DID NOT come back for another lesson in sign language, nor did Luke come by for another chat that day. Even Ted, who came up to deliver food, didn't stick around to chat today, leaving Max alone to try and piece together what happened that morning.

Maybe he was just really good at charades. Luke managed to mime everything out so clearly that he was able to understand exactly what he was talking about, even though his movements were clumsy and his fingers didn't always move right. Maybe Luke did something himself to help Max understand what he was saying. He didn't know why Ally thought something was going on with it.

He let his attention drift to trying to read a book, then when he couldn't bring himself to care about that, to figuring out what to do about his leg. Everyone else seemed to be healing up fine, but he was still bedridden and turning all sorts of colours he shouldn't be. There was too much wrong with his body for him to concentrate on fixing one thing, but damn if he'd spend much longer lying in this bed. His leg needed to be fixed.

He knew what his leg was supposed to look and feel like. It shouldn't feel like his bones were being held together by scotch tape, but like they were all in one piece. His muscles shouldn't feel like they were on fire with every movement. His skin should definitely not be any shades of yellow, green, blue, purple or black. He should be able to walk and swim on it. It shouldn't feel like it was on fire every time it moved.

"Max? You okay?"

Max jumped at the voice and looked madly around the room. Jaime appeared at the end of the bed, watching him. "Oh," Max said. "Hey."

"Ally and Ted are kind of going conspiracy theory downstairs," she said. "What the fuck did you do?"

"I've just been sitting here," Max said. "I can barely get to the washroom on my own. What do you think I've been doing?"

"They think you've been holding back and you can do a lot more than you've let on." Jaime was calm and far more curious than accusing.

Max stumbled through the idea. More than he let on? More than what, exactly? He didn't even know what was happening lately, instead just hoping that it would make sense eventually.

A couple weeks ago he was in high school and now he was able to heal the injured. His leg was fixing itself painfully slowly, but still faster than it had any right to. Nothing made any sense yet.

If anything, they were keeping more from him than he was from them. He still didn't know where they were heading or what the plan was. They couldn't really just be moving from house to house, intent on hiding for the rest of their lives. He didn't even know who these people after them were or what they wanted.

"It's like Mary all over again," Jaime muttered rubbing the back of her head. "Just stop doing that."

"Stop what?"

"*Thinking*," she said, shutting her eyes tight before opening them again. "At least I figured out why you and Luke can talk to each other and are probably getting along so well."

"You lost — wait, what did you say?"

Jaime sat on the bed, her weight barely shifting the covers. "Okay, so—"

"Who's Mary?" Max asked.

"No one you know."

"But Harrison knows who she is."

"No, he doesn't."

"He said something about Mary and Jack before I got my leg broken in two."

Jaime frowned, but didn't look at him. "Okay, so he doesn't *usually* know who they are. It's best if we keep it that way."

"And Ally thinks *I'm* keeping secrets. Who were they?"

Jaime shook her head. "It was a while back. I can barely remember them myself. Mary, she could move things with her mind, but then she just started to buzz after a while. Luke used to do it too, back when they first found me and picked me up. When Luke was really thinking about something or freaking out, there was always this buzz you could feel in your head. It took me a while to figure out what it was, but it was Luke. He doesn't do it much anymore, but you don't forget that feeling."

"And you're saying I'm buzzing?"

"Yep. Pretty annoying."

"And...?"

"And what?"

"And what am I supposed to do about it?"

"I don't know," Jaime said. "Stop thinking so damn loud?"

Max glowered at her for the complete lack of help before snapping his head to the closed door. Harrison appeared there a moment later and Jaime let out a snort. "He does that too. All the time."

"Oh," Harrison said, looking at Jaime.

"You were never here," Jaime said, not even turning around to look at him.

Max looked back and forth between them. "This is about Harrison encouraging me to go wander off or something, right?" he asked.

They both shot him a look and Max put up his hands. "No one said anything. I just kind of figured. Since every time the two of us leave the house, something bad happens…"

Silence hung in the room and Max hoped they wouldn't try to call him on his explanation. He wasn't sure where it had come from. He had no idea why Harrison hadn't come by or what was going on outside of this room. The reasoning just came to him and, from the looks on both of their faces, he was right.

"Right," Jaime said, though she didn't seem to believe Max. Jaime looked him over like he was a memory that she wasn't sure she should keep.

"I'm sorry about what happened," Harrison said, ignoring it entirely. "There was no way to know that they would find us like that. Which probably means nothing considering everything."

"It's okay," Max told him. "Time to reflect, right?" Harrison didn't look so convinced, but Max had something else on his mind now that Harrison was here. "How well do you remember that night?"

"Before or after I hit my head?"

"After, I think," Max said, trying to bring the scene up again. "The woman in the white suit. Did she look weird to you?"

Harrison thought back. "I don't think I saw anything weird about her," he said. "I was seeing about twelve of everything after I banged my head into that post. Or I got thrown into it. Why?"

"I don't think she was wearing the shades," Max said. "I swear it looked like she had red eyes. You know, like Luke and Willow's. And she was dressed like Willow."

"You sure you were seeing things right?"

"I don't know," he said, shaking his head. "This whole thing is messed up."

"Are we getting close to Hope?" Jaime asked. At the confused looks, she rolled her eyes. "Vancouver."

"I think the next place we're heading is somewhere near Washington," Max said. "It might be Vancouver."

"This has something to do with Rue," Jaime said. She stared down at the floor, but looked like she was looking much further down than the carpet. "Don't ask. I could never get it out of them, even when they were chatty."

"Luke's coming," Max said.

Jaime looked at Harrison, who promptly vanished. She then turned to Max and said quietly and quickly, "Find out what's going on. Luke might be a little more willing to talk. He always was the one who actually seemed to want us around."

"Tell me more about Mary."

Jaime nodded and vanished.

Luke appeared seconds later, meeting Max's eyes with a smile on his face. *Not moving yet,* he said. *We found a better place, though.*

"Where are we going?" he started.

Washington, Luke signed. Max realized his signs were more like him flapping his arms around a bit and trying to make his fingers move with them.

"You said we were getting closer to something, right?" Max asked. A hundred other little questions battled in his mind to get out. "That thing is in Washington?"

Luke looked at him and shook his head. *No, the gate's up in Hope. We still have a little while before we get there. You should be better by the time we make it up that far.*

Hope. Like what Jaime said earlier. "What's in Hope?"

Luke hesitated, looking like he didn't want to talk about it. Maybe Willow had told him not to do it, since she seemed to be all for withholding information. It probably wasn't for any malicious reason, just worry that it would frighten all of them and they might think they could run off on their own. And if they ran off on their own, well, look at what happened to Max. He wasn't going to be responsible for all of them ending up like Max if he could help it.

Max stopped at the realization that he was thinking of himself in the third person.

"It's all right," Max insisted. "What am I going to do? Run?"

Willow appeared in the room and didn't even bother looking at Max, turning right on Luke with her arms folded. Her back looked like it was doing much better.

You know he's just humouring you, right?

It wasn't clear, but Max could definitely tell exactly what Willow was saying even without her hands moving.

I've been getting a lot better, Luke told her. *You were just a bad teacher.*

Your hands barely move, Luke, she reminded him. *When we get to the other side, we'll be able to get you some new ones and then you'll be able to actually learn. Right now, he's got no idea what you're saying.*

He asked about where we're going. They deserve to know what's going on. We've just been leading them around for so long and keeping them safe, but they don't know what's coming.

And what happened the last time we told them what was coming? Mary and Jack? They ran away and Emma got them, you remember? Both of them joined her and now Emma's coming back after the rest of them. And if we didn't keep stopping to collect them all, then maybe we'd already be through the gate.

It's not what Rue would have wanted.

And there was that name. Rue. He had no idea what it meant and he could barely even process that it had come up. The words came so quickly that he had trouble following.

Rue wanted to bring everyone over to the other side, Willow, Luke continued. *Just because they're after us doesn't mean that they aren't going to keep doing the same thing to the rest of them. They're still collecting them, too. We can save them. We can bring them with us.*

I'm not having this argument again. I let you keep finding them and letting them tag along. You can keep as many of them as you want. But we don't have to tell them any of it. They'll figure it out on the other side anyway.

They should know who is after them, Luke insisted. *And where we're going.*

Fine, she said. *Tell him. But I don't think he can understand anything you're saying. Not really. Look at him. Completely spaced out. He's probably fallen asleep.*

Willow took one last look at Max before vanishing.

Max didn't register the comment, latching on to other bits of the conversation. Pieces of that almost made sense while other bits left him lost and he struggled to keep track of which was which. There was someone named Rue who wanted them to go to a place where everything would be better. There was also someone named Emma that they didn't like.

This was beyond asking what was in Hope.

It was the wind of the hand passing over his face that snapped him back to attention. "What? Sorry," he said, shaking his head and hoping that his thoughts would fall into place inside of the jumble. "What was that about?"

She doesn't want me telling you guys anything. She thinks it's going to scare you guys off.

"Why would it scare us off?" Max asked, sure to repeat part of his response in his question so he knew that he understood him. It was probably a bad idea to mention he had heard their conversation.

It's a bit of a long story.

"I'm not really going anywhere."

Luke smiled. *The people who are after you, he began, his hands moving slowly as he tried to figure out what he was trying to say, we have a bit of history. They go around trying to find kids like us. Psychics, they call them. And they bring them all to their lab in the middle of nowhere and do lots of experiments on them to make them like... well, us. They're still looking for people, so we're trying to find them before they do.*

"So the suit guys," Max repeated, trying to get it straight, "they're after us because we have these powers? But none of us can do nearly the things you guys can."

They can make you do all of it. They have ways. Luke looked a little distracted and Max got flashes of blood and pain. Electric shocks. Crying and screams in the night. Arms being severed. Lab coats. Legs left still attached but mangled. Drowning. Flames. Being buried alive. Prosthetic limbs that you either learned to move or you just didn't get to move at all.

Luke snapped out of it quickly. *We managed to escape. Just a few of us. It wasn't really the best idea, though. Once we got out, there wasn't really anywhere we could go. People don't respond well to people who can't talk and who can make things move with their minds and stuff. It freaked them out.*

The problem, really, was that there was only one place that we were meant to be. See, in the facility there's a gate. Rue — she was the oldest and she's the one who got us out — she used to tell us all about the gate and what was on the other side. She'd seen it. She made it through once and they pulled her back. There's a place there that is made up of lots of people like us. It's like a paradise and it's where we're supposed to be. But they're guarding the gate now and we were trying not to get too close to them.

Max could almost see the gate. Buried deep in the darkness at the end of a tunnel carved out of the dirt with a stone floor, there was a golden gate that shone from the interlacing golden weave. On the other side, there were whites and pastels and the vaguest hints of things moving that he could not quite make out, as well as a sense of calm and relaxation. He hadn't even seen it with his own eyes and he wanted to go.

We were supposed to go back there. We split up. Willow and I, we weren't ready to go back yet. The labs were terrifying. Instead, we started trying to find all the kids that the people from the labs were going after and trying to warn them, but there were always lab people right on our tails. So we had to start taking them so they wouldn't get caught.

"Willow doesn't seem that into keeping us around."

That's because some of them left. And when they left, they ended up getting caught by Emma. She used to be one of us, but she went back and they caught her again. She's one of them now. She can track other kids down, the same as me. She's the one that's been trying to track down me and Willow and trying to get all of you guys.

"Okay," Max said, just trying to keep this all straight. "And Rue is..."

Rue was the oldest. She knew everything. She said that if we ever got out, we should try to keep other kids like us from ever getting caught again and we should try and save as many as we could. She sacrificed herself to let us escape, but she still managed to throw herself into the gate in the end. She's waiting for us on the other side.

Max believed him. He wanted to believe that Rue was really there just on the other side. She was the big sister he'd never had, someone he could look up to in times of pain and bloodshed. In the darkest times, she'd be there for him, like she was there for everyone.

Do me a favour? Luke asked. *Tell the others. But try to make it so that they don't run away. Willow doesn't really take it very well when she thinks people are trying to run away. Not since the last time.*

"Sure," Max said, and Luke was gone. He sat there for a while, just trying to process everything. They were heading to a facility that focused on torturing psychic kids until they exhibited as many powers as Luke and Willow had in ways that would result in death and more pain than Max thought he probably would ever experience. They wanted to risk it to get through a gate with the promise of paradise on the other side of it. He wasn't sure why but he believed it all, though there was a lingering nagging sense of doubt in the back of his mind. It thought something seemed funny about the story, but he couldn't find the hole in it.

And Rue. He could almost picture her, a young woman all in white, no older than the rest of them, her eyes also red and her hair white. She would help them and she would take them all to the place where they would be happy if only they would trust her.

And then there was Emma, the traitor who went over to the other side. She now replaced the woman in white in his memories, ordering the death of his parents and breaking his leg. It was her there in that moment right before Harrison got them back to that street where they were living at the time. She wasn't the woman in white in that moment. She was just a girl and she looked genuinely concerned.

"Max, stop that," Jaime said, grabbing him by the shoulder

and shaking him. The room was dark now, night having settled in. He wondered how long he'd been sitting there like that. "What happened?"

"There was a lot," Max said running his palm over his temple. "We're heading to Washington next on our way to Hope. And I know who Rue is. And who the woman in the white is. And just, a lot of stuff."

"You look like shit," Jaime said, leaving through the door. "Get some sleep. We'll talk later."

CHAPTER FOURTEEN

IT WAS TOO hot in here and Max was too wired from the conversation with Luke to sleep. His mind was spinning as he tried to sift through the images and thoughts, unable to force them to make sense. They were hard to even focus on. He needed a distraction.

There had to be a TV somewhere in the house. He could deal with a bit of static if it would get his mind off of everything.

Pain shot up through his leg as soon as he tried to bend it, but he forced himself out of bed and to the door. His leg wasn't ready to put weight on yet and he could feel the bone strain and bend under him as he leaned against the bed, then the wall, trying to shuffle his way out of the room. It was holding up better than he thought it would, but he would be happy once he was off of it again.

There were stairs just outside of his room and he sat on the top step, lowering himself step by step. His leg would jostle, but it didn't hurt nearly as much as stepping on it. He went slow, already feeling winded from the short walk and he could feel himself falling asleep.

"Hey. Hey! Max?"

Max woke to someone shaking his shoulder. He groaned and looked up to Harrison. His stormy grey eyes looked worried and Max blinked up at him. His back was sore and he realized he had fallen asleep sitting up and slumped against the wall. He was on the stairs, his leg aching below him on the steps.

Right. Trying to find the TV.

"You okay? What happened?"

"I was looking for TV," Max said. "It is really boring lying in bed all day."

Harrison smiled at him and shook his head. "I'm starting to think you're a dumbass," he said. He took Max by the hand and got him up to his feet, putting his arm over his shoulders. "You could have just asked me, you know."

They appeared in a living room with a television and Harrison helped Max down onto the couch. Max sank into the cushions and put his leg up on the coffee table. He was almost used to this appearing in random places thing. "Sure," he said. "I'll be sure to ask whenever I see you."

Harrison sank into the couch next to him. "I'm sorry, by the way. Just, for everything."

"It's fine," Max said. "No way you could have known. I just can't leave the house anymore."

"They got a Playstation," Harrison said. "Unfortunately, I already tried and the controllers don't connect."

"Of course not," Max said. He wondered if it actually didn't connect or if he didn't see it. He still needed to ask Jaime if she could see anything through the static or if it was just him. He didn't want to ask Harrison, not sure what he'd say if he couldn't see anything. Granted, he hadn't looked at a television since that first night he showed up here, so he wasn't sure if he could still see anything through the static himself.

"Hey, do you feel that?" Harrison asked, rubbing at the back of his head and looking around like there was a fly circling his head. "Max? Max!"

"What?" Max asked, snapping out of his reverie and back to Harrison. He recognized that look from Jaime last night. "Sorry. I'm just kind of... Sorry. I forgot. Trying to not do the whole..." his finger moved in a circle around his head in a wavering, uncertain manner, "... thing?"

"It's you?"

"I think so? Jaime said I was doing something last night. I'm not really sure what's going on or how to stop it—"

"No," Harrison said quickly. "No, it's all right. If anyone's going to understand about this, it's us. We know it's not intentional. It's just kind of... what exactly is happening?"

"I don't really know. I'm buzzing or something. And I can understand what Luke's signing even though he's just waving his hands around. I just kind of know what he wants to say when he does it."

"That sounds a bit like you're reading minds."

"Shouldn't I be hearing stuff from everyone all the time, then?"

Harrison shrugged, though he looked nervous. "Maybe you need to focus on it to pick anything up. Like, you're trying to talk to Luke, so you pick up Luke, right? And right now, are... you getting anything?"

"Do you want me to try to get anything?" he asked slowly.

Harrison hesitated. "It's not that I don't trust you, I just..."

"I don't really know how to do it if I wanted to. I don't think I've done it so far, so I'm just going to not try doing it at all. I'm already in enough trouble with you guys."

"You're not in that much trouble. I mean, you're probably going to get Ally pissed when she realizes you got out of your room..."

"Do you know how boring it is staring at a wall all day?"

"Jaime's mentioned it, yeah," Harrison said with a bit of

a laugh. "You remember, she was kind of stuck in your position when you first got here?"

"Yeah, good times," he said.

Silence lingered in the air between the two of them. Max looked around for the remote, hoping the static could break it, but he couldn't see it anywhere. Outside, the early morning sun streamed in, but it was much cooler here than in his room.

"Do you ever think about home?" Max asked, needing to fill the silence before his mind started to wander again. "Like, what if you ever went back and just went back to school and all that? What would you have done if all this hadn't happened?"

Harrison leaned back and let his eyes drift up to the ceiling. "I don't know," he said. "College? I never thought that far ahead. Maybe law school or get into government work or something. Maybe. I could have tried being in a band. Some video game design thing? I could be a tester. It'd be a lot more fun than being stuck in an office doing paperwork."

Max nodded. "I didn't know either," he said. "I was going to be a lifeguard for the summer and after that, keep up with school and hope something hit me. Try to keep Tara from setting me up with every girl she thought liked me."

"What do you mean, try?" Harrison asked.

"I'm..." he hesitated. "I don't know, I was never really interested in any of them. I just didn't really want a girlfriend with everything else. School. Lifeguard training. I didn't have time."

Hopeful and smug were the two things that radiated from Harrison and Max wasn't sure why.

"Take your time," Harrison said instead. "I'm sure someone will come along."

"What about—"

"Max!" Ally called from elsewhere in the house.

Harrison stiffened beside him. "She is going to kick the shit out of me if she catches me talking to you," he said. "Sorry."

Harrison was gone a moment later. Max frowned at the spot he'd been sitting as he heard Ally moving around somewhere else on the same floor, opening and closing doors.

Sure. Ask you any time for a hand.

Max continued his search for the remote until Ally appeared in the doorway. Whatever words she had died on her lips as she looked in awe at him as he finally managed to pull a remote out of the couch cushions. He pointed it at the television and hit the power button. Absolutely nothing happened.

"Hey," he said, frowning at the remote. "How's it going?"

"You aren't supposed to be up! Why aren't you in bed?"

"I haven't been up for a week," Max told her. "I took a walk. This is as far as I got."

"But your leg—"

"Is getting better," Max told her. "A lot better, and I don't want to forget how to walk. It's not like I can get very far and I'm certainly not going off running anywhere on it yet," he added, seeing that she was getting worried. "I'm pretty sure I need to get up once in a while so I don't forget how to use my legs all together."

Ally took in a breath and let the arguments she had rest. She came over to perch on the armrest of the couch and faced him. "You're not just healing anymore, are you?" she asked.

"What?"

"I've been thinking about it. The whole knowing people are coming before they show up and the being able to read that obviously not sign language thing Luke's doing—"

"You think I can read minds?"

"No, I — can you?"

Max shook his head quickly. "Not that I know of."

Ally leaned back away from him. "I was just going to say that maybe your healing powers are getting stronger and giving off weird side effects, but, if you're reading minds now—"

"No! No mind reading." Max could tell she was nervous, but couldn't think of anything to make it better.

"Hey, you found the cripple," Ted said, walking in. "The mind reading cripple?"

"Nope," Max insisted. "No idea what either of you are thinking right now or—"

"What about just a little bit of mind reading?" Ted asked. "Or maybe a bit of an empath thing. It might explain how he can understand Luke and he just knows when people are going to show up. I would kill to have an actual psychic in the house."

"Shouldn't you be making breakfast?" Ally asked.

"I think it's your turn this time," Ted said.

Right about now, Max would take any excuse for Ally to stop asking him about mind reading. He stayed still, watching Ally as she frowned at Ted. The moment lasted for a moment too long before she finally got up. "Fine," she said, walking out of the room.

"Huh," Ted said, watching her go. He turned back and gave Max a knowing look and a smile. "That never works."

Max shrugged and began his hunt for a second, working remote. He could already tell Ted was convinced he developed some kind of mind reading ability, and the fact that Max knew that meant that he might be right. To Max, though, it was just another thing that he didn't know he was doing and didn't want to think too much about.

Ted took a seat on the floor beside him, his eyes on Max's leg and the bruising that covered it. "So how bored were you to try walking on that thing?"

"You ever had to lie down in a room for a week solid? That bored."

"But you're still pretty good at healing yourself now, right? Leg notwithstanding."

"I am not going to like your next question."

"You can see the future too?" Ted asked. When Max didn't react, he cracked a smile. "So have you heard of blood ben—"

"No," Max said. He hadn't seen Avatar in years and couldn't quite remember the mechanics of blood bending beyond using the other person's blood to control their body, but that was enough.

"Come on, it's not like you have anything else to do. Just a little? Just once? Just to see if I can."

"You can't be serious."

"If it doesn't work, I'll drop the whole thing."

"I can't even walk."

"So I'll just try to move your hand a little."

"Why do you want to do this so badly?"

"Because do you know how cool it would be?" Ted immediately rethought that statement and brought down the excitement on his face and out of his voice. "And think about it. If something happens and Willow isn't around to kick some ass, what am I going to do? Splash water in their faces? Or am I going to figure out a way to make them walk right back out the door?"

Max hesitated before he offered his hand. This was a horrible idea and he knew it. "Just once," he said. "One time. *That's it.*"

Ted looked as excited as a five year old on Christmas morning. He turned to Max's hand, now resting beside him on the couch, and forced himself to concentrate. His brows furrowed and Max waited for this decision to backfire.

It took Max less than thirty seconds to lose the feeling in his hand. He couldn't move it and it went numb quickly. The pain followed in sharp twitches as the muscles tried to move on their own, lifting his fingers. "Stop!" he yelled as it started to cramp through the numbness. "Stop!"

Ted physically backed away as he released control of the blood in his hand. "What happened? I thought it was working."

Max massaged his hand and tried to get the circulation back. His wrist was bruised and he turned back to Ted. "Blood needs to *move*," he told Ted, flexing his fingers. "You moved my fingers, but you kind of stopped the circulation." He rubbed his hand over his wrist and the bruising faded away.

"I don't think I'm going to be able to try this with anyone else," Ted said, his eyes on Max's wrist.

"I am the only one in this place stupid enough to let you screw around with the blood that's still inside me," Max agreed. "Let me guess. You want to try just one more time?"

"What the hell is going on in here?" Ally demanded, coming back into the room. "Ted trying to convince you to do that blood thing?"

"It kinda worked."

"You *let* him?"

Willow appeared in the middle of the room, looking around at the three of them. Max noticed that she took the effort to glower at him before moving on to Ally. She moved her hands in very quick, precise movements, and Max could tell that she was doing this on Luke's request. *We're moving in ten minutes.*

"*You know sign language?*" Ally demanded. Willow looked entirely unimpressed and vanished again. Ally turned on Ted and Max. "You're telling me she could communicate *all this time*? Did you know?"

"I think Jaime mentioned it once," Ted said.

"How could Willow never just tell me? I've been trying to teach her and she already knows!"

"Well, you are kind of bossy," Ted said. "Did you piss her off when you met her?"

"That's no excuse!"

"So you did do something."

"It was *not* that bad!" she exclaimed. "I was just..."

"Wait, if we're leaving soon, where are Jaime and Harrison?"

"Luke's probably out getting them," Ted said. "Lucky bastards get to go out and wander all they want all day."

"You could go with them, you know," Ally said. "Let me have a quiet house for once."

"And miss the chance to practice bloodbending with Max? I don't think so."

"Who said I'm letting you do that again?" Max asked.

"Aw, come on," Ted said, getting up. "I helped you get better at healing. Look at how fast you fixed your hand up! I could probably teach you to be a better empath too, in exchange for a little practice."

"No."

"Think on it," he said. "And if you will excuse me, I need to shove all my stuff into my bag before we move."

Max stared after him, confused. "What..."

"Right, you haven't exactly been conscious for a lot of the moves so far," Ally said, returning to her perch on the couch. "When we move places, Luke and Willow bring our backpacks along with us. If we don't have everything in there, though, we're not getting it back. Should probably get you a backpack at the next place. And maybe some new clothes."

She eyed Max and Max already knew why. He had been in the same shirt and pants for over a week. It was the only thing he had. He didn't even have shoes, those lost back in the pink room as near as he could tell. He'd barely noticed that he had nothing until now, but he knew he shouldn't stay in the same thing for much longer. There were sweat, blood and food stains all over him and he could probably do with a shower as well as a new shirt at this point.

Max let out a grunt of pain as his leg dropped to the ground. The coffee table was gone and the room had changed again. Light streamed in from behind him through large windows and the screen in front of him got a lot smaller. It was now a flat screen hanging above a stone fireplace. On the mantle were family photos, one of the kids in them looking about Max's size. Once he found his room, Max was stealing a change of clothing.

Ally dropped to the ground, catching herself before she landed and rolling out of it. "That was not ten minutes," she muttered, looking around. "Oh, that's different."

"What's different?" Max asked.

Ally pointed out the windows. Max turned around, wincing as he moved his leg to look. Out back, there was a large above ground pool, currently covered, surrounded by trees. There was a deck off to one side of it and a diving board, but Max was more concerned if it was filled.

Finally, something familiar. He would let Ted do all the blood-bending he wanted if it meant that he could heal fast enough to get in that pool.

CHAPTER FIFTEEN

HOW IS YOUR LEG? Ally asked, her hands moving to sign it at Max.

Max brought up his hands and tried to remember what any of the signs that Ally had taught him today were. He couldn't remember *sore, better than usual, less like I want to cut it off than normal* or *good enough for you to let me go in the damn pool*. She may not have taught him all of those.

"We *just* went over this, Max," Ally said. "Don't make me regret getting you all that stuff."

Max frowned looking at the backpack, filled with clothing with the tags still on it. He was starting to think it was more of a bribe than a gift at this point.

"Hey," Ted said, dropping in behind Max with a towel over his shoulder wearing swim trunks. "Max, do the thing we practiced."

"What thing?" Ally asked.

Max nodded and put up his hands. He met Ally's eyes and

flicked them, pushing a thought from his mind into hers. What-ever his hands were doing, that was the sign for *Sore*. He was say-ing *Sore*.

"You taught him to say sore?" Ally asked, looking up at Ted.

"I taught him how to make you *think* he said sore," Ted said, clapping Max on the shoulder. "Good job, padawan. One of these days, you will earn some pool time."

Max glared at him as he left out the back door to the pool. When he looked back, Ally had her arms crossed and did not look happy with him.

"I don't know what you did, but don't do that. I don't want anyone in my head."

"Sorry," Max said, though he knew she wasn't that angry with him. Instead there was a sense of disappointment that didn't bother Max at all. He didn't know why he needed to learn sign lan-guage if he could practically hear everything someone was signing at him.

Ally seemed satisfied with that and left, leaving Max alone with his leg. It had improved significantly over the last couple days. Max assumed it was a combination of the bone finally prop-erly fusing in his calf and his sheer determination to be well enough to get in the pool. He could limp around the first floor now and even managed to go out into the backyard to dip his hands into the pool, but the steps were still painful and his insistence that swimming would be good physiotherapy for him fell on deaf ears.

He went for the remote on the couch next to him, only to find it not working again. The strangest part of this house was the fact that the remote batteries kept disappearing. He'd had to scrounge to find replacements for them three times in the last two days.

This time, however, the reason they were gone was clear. When he looked back up at the screen, Jaime stood there with the batteries in her hands and smiling at him. "Time to play catch up," she said. "What the hell did Luke tell you?"

"Hello to you too." Max looked around, finding the pair of them alone for the moment. "You sure you want to do this here and now? Someone might walk in."

"Ted's in the pool, Ally's looking for her book and Luke and Willow are off looking for the next place after this. What did he say?"

Max watched her take a seat on the couch next to him and he handed her the remote. He tried to think back. "Luke said he wanted me to tell everyone, but it all sounds a bit nuts. The people after us want to take us and do experiments on us to make us like Luke and Willow. I think they're leading us back to them so we can go through some gate. There was something about someone named Rue, too..."

"Rue," Jaime repeated. She knew the name, nodding along.

"They've mentioned her before. Used to talk about her a lot more when Mary was around."

"Who is Mary?" Max asked. "They said something about Jack and Mary getting freaked out when they told them about this."

"It's... fuzzy," Jaime said. Her eyes found a spot on the floor and stared at it, concentrating so the words would continue to come out. "Mary was kind of like you. She buzzed sometimes and she understood everyone, even when they didn't say anything. She knew right away when Ally showed up that we were related. And then she talked to Luke and she said something about a gate. I can't remember what it was about that gate..."

"Harrison," Max said.

Harrison appeared in the room, looking from the pair of them on the couch to the television. "Not watching static?" he asked. "I thought you guys loved the... you okay?"

Jaime shook her head and tore her eyes up from the spot on the floor. She leaned back on the couch, arms crossed and remote in her lap. "Fine."

"Why do I get the feeling I interrupted something?"

"We were just continuing that talk from a few nights ago," Max said.

"Oh." Harrison dropped onto the couch beside Max, careful to avoid bumping into his leg and turned to look at both of them. "In that case, I've been trying to think of why they seem to find us everytime Max leaves the house. I can't be the only one who's noticed they're getting more aggressive and it's only with him."

"Luke said something about that," Max said. "Apparently they're just finding me. Something about me is easy to track down when I'm away from you guys."

"Mary too," Jaime muttered, her eyes back on that spot on the ground. Harrison looked at her, but didn't seem to have heard her say anything.

"Wouldn't it be easier to find a whole bunch of us?" Harrison asked. "I remember they used to track us down a lot until, like, Texas or something."

Mary. Max could hear the name radiating off of Jaime and she kept staring at that spot on the carpet, trying desperately to remember more than she could. Max shifted uncomfortably away from her, not sure what to do to help.

"What are you even doing here?" Max asked. "Aren't you usually out of the house most of the time?"

"Ally wanted to do a run," he said. "I'll go find her in a bit."

"What do you even do when you go out?" he asked. "There can't be that much stuff around here."

"Check out wherever we are," Harrison said. "See the museums. Catch a movie. Check out some of the stuff they've got locally. Try not to get caught. Anything but just sit around here waiting until we move again."

"Wait, movie?"

Harrison stopped. "Forget I said that," he said quickly. "I didn't say that."

"Sure," Max said, smiling.

"You're going to make me take you to a movie, aren't you?"

"Or you can help me get to the pool," Max said. "Luke and Willow are already looking for a new place. We might as well enjoy the pool before it's gone, right?"

Harrison looked down at the bruising still covering Max's leg. "Are you sure?"

"Swimming is *great* physiotherapy," Max insisted. "It should help me get better faster."

"Says the guy who's letting Ted practice bloodbending on him."

"He's getting better," Max said, his hand reflexively massaging his palm and fingers from the memories. "He doesn't quite understand blood flow yet, though. Too fast, then too slow, then forgetting about it all together and forgetting that it's sometimes new blood and not the same blood and reversing the flow of it sometimes... He's getting better."

"You are an idiot for letting him try that on you."

"He's been showing me how to do stuff too. Quid pro quo. Now, about giving me a hand outside..."

"Take off the brace first," Jaime said. "That's not going to last wet."

"Do not tell Ally I'm doing this," Harrison said. He watched as Max removed the tape from the makeshift splint, still made of the same two sticks of wood as before. The tape peeled off in pieces, taking strands of his leg hair with it, but Max tore through it until he was free. He flexed his foot and managed to keep his wincing in check.

"Hey Max?" Ally called down the stairs. "Jaime? Have you seen Harrison?"

Harrison looked panicked as he turned to Max, arms outstretched, and took him by the shoulders. "You're positive?"

"Yeah."

"You can definitely swim."

"Yes."

He was no longer sitting on a couch, but falling through the water. He let out a yelp of surprise before his head fell under the surface. It was blissfully cold, but his mouth filled with the mild tang of chlorine and he pulled himself back up.

Water in his eyes, he took a deep breath of air and looked around as best he could. He wiped the water and hair off his face and looked around, finding Ted grinning at him. He turned back around to Harrison, still dry as he stood on the deck and smiling.

"Ally never finds out about this," Harrison said before he vanished. Max wasn't sure if he was talking to him or Ted.

"About time you showed up," Ted said, laughing.

Max went for the edge. His clothes were a bit too heavy for him to manage and he took off his soaked shirt to lighten the load. He could see Ted coming up behind him with every intention of dunking him and Max dropped back down into the water. Using his good leg, he pushed off the side of the pool and swam around him, out into the open water.

Max could already feel the pull of something in the pool, a gentle current that was quickly picking up steam. Max took another breath and looked around, Ted now sitting on the diving board and swirling his finger in the air as the water moved in the same fashion.

He had no intention of going towards the ledge. He had just gotten in the water. Ted wasn't going to hurt him, so Max continued swimming like the whirlpool wasn't there, his arms aching from lack of practice, but his bad leg not hurting nearly as much as it did when he tried to walk.

Ted was saying something as the current got stronger, but Max couldn't hear it with the water in his ears. He kept trying to fight it, to keep himself above the pull of the waves, but it became too much. Pain shot through his good leg as it seized up, the cramp spreading down through the bottom of his foot, and he was pulled under the waves.

The water stopped moving around him before he hit the bottom of the pool. Max let himself drift down to the bottom and kicked himself up, grabbing the side of the pool and leaning over it. He coughed the water out of his lungs.

"Max, I'm so sorry," Ted said, swimming over to him. "Are you okay?"

Max coughed up enough to manage a laugh. The smile across his face was so strong he didn't know if he'd be able to stop. "That was awesome!"

Ted looked relieved as he took a spot next to Max on the ledge. "Hey, you're a pretty good swimmer."

"I was training to be a lifeguard," Max told him. "I kind of had to be."

"You want to see how good?" Ted smiled and Max could feel the pull of a current forming in the water.

"Not right now," Max said. "Maybe when my leg isn't bruised to hell and I can actually walk on it."

"You're not as fun as I hoped, you know that?"

Max pushed off the ledge back into the pool. "You're just going to have to find someone else to drown," he told Ted before he dove back under the water.

There was that feeling again, hitting him like lightning. Someone was out there and looking for him, but it was wrong. They shouldn't be trying to find him here. He was still at the house with... just Ted nearby to mask him.

Max broke the surface and looked frantically for Ted. "We have to go," he said, making for the deck. "Someone's coming."

"What?"

"Come *on*," he said. Ted followed him out and put Max's arm over his shoulder, helping him limp back into the house. He stopped Ted at the door and looked between it and the pool. "You think you could freeze the door over with the pool water? You know, so no one can get in?"

"Maybe?" Ted said. He got the pair of them inside and brought the pool water over the door in a solid block and narrowed his eyes. His hands moved in front of him and the water slowly froze. "What the hell do you think is about to happen?"

Ted turned back once he was done and stopped, looking at something behind Max. His eyes widened and he flew across the room, over the couch into the dine-in kitchen and skidding across the floor.

Max turned to see a man in shades and a black suit. Max's first impulse was for the door, but it was stuck now and he instead tried to limp to Ted.

"Do something!" Ted yelled at him.

"Like what? *Think* at them?"

Something grabbed him from behind and he was pulled back towards the man in the suit. He knew Jaime was coming, but he never saw if she made it back downstairs. The room vanished around him.

CHAPTER SIXTEEN

MAX WAS STILL freaking out when the flashes of places stopped. There were flashes of alleys and empty fields and abandoned gymnasiums, none of which he cared about as much as his inability to move or make a sound. When they stopped, he was in a long white hallway with the guy in the suit, hovering a foot off the ground and still unable to move. Max tried to make a sound, but he couldn't even manage that.

A sound echoed down the hallway, faint but definitely there. Max could tell someone was coming. The man in the suit quickly opened the door to his right and put Max down in there, shutting it immediately after him.

"Hey!" Max yelled, limping back to the door. He banged on it helplessly, his cries being heard by no one. There was no one out there for him.

Max let out a breath and looked around the room. There was nothing in here but a bed and a small table. There was another door that had been left open, but it lead only to the bathroom. There was a panel of glass on one wall, covered by a white sheet of metal.

Any ability he had to remain calm quickly escaped him. He sunk down in the corner of the room, his mind racing as he tried to put together what happened. The man in black had grabbed him from inside the house and now he was locked inside a room that he couldn't escape from. He was probably inside the facility where they did those experiments.

He went back through the things Luke had passed on to him. The pain. The fear. They grabbed him so easily and he was stuck here now. They'd find some way to make him like Luke and Willow and tear off his arms to make him learn.

He needed to get out. There had to be a way out.

"Okay kid, there's no way I was ever this bad." The door opened and there was a girl standing there, no older than Harrison with wavy black hair and olive skin. Max tried to scramble to his feet to rush the door, but she held out her hand, Max falling back and once more unable to struggle out of an invisible grip.

"Holy crap, what did Adam do to you?" she asked, looking down at his leg. She shook her head and met his eyes again. "Look, you need to calm the fuck down or this plan isn't working."

Max felt whatever was holding him lift off of his mouth.

"Who are you?" Max asked, unable to keep the panic out of his voice. "What do you want?"

The other girl rolled her eyes. "Name's Mary. I used to travel with Luke and Willow, too. And *I* want everyone to admit that this is a terrible fucking plan."

Max stared at her, one thing sticking in his mind. *Mary.* This was the other girl, the one Luke and Willow said had left before. The one Jaime seemed to know but struggled so hard to remember.

"What everyone *else* wants," she continued, "is to stage a big rescue and stop Luke and Willow before they decide to fulfill that old suicide pact of theirs. I'm going to tell you this now, though. Your best bet is to just walk away from this whole thing. You do not need to be the hero."

"They said the woman in white got you," Max said. "There was something about experiments and—"

"No," Mary said, taking a seat in front of him. He felt the invisible grip on him loosen and he made no move to run as she settled down. "I mean, I have Adam now, but that's not really that big of a deal anymore. And technically the woman in white did get me, but, well..."

The sentence hovered in the air for a very long moment before the woman in white appeared behind Mary. Max backed up against the wall and felt the invisible grip hold him still again.

Mary took a breath and met his eyes as the woman stood there, staying against the other wall and watching.

"Okay, let's start this terrible idea."

Just do it, the woman said, her hands moving in one, short burst.

"Okay, kid," Mary said, the expression on her face telling him that she thought this was a stupid idea. "I want you to look at her. *Really* look at her."

He didn't have much choice in the matter. He couldn't move his head away. The woman stood there, dressed in a white pant suit and sunglasses, arms crossed and glaring at him over Mary's shoulder.

The silence lingered and he continued to look until he started to see something else. She was still there, looking harshly at him like she was trying to decide the best way to sever his arms, but there was also a version of her that was holding her arms in front of her chest, looking at him with concern in her red eyes. This version of her was dressed in black, in a style closer to what Willow regularly wore.

"You're seeing her twice, right?" Mary asked. "White suit and in a black skirt and corset combo?"

Max's eyes shot to Mary, demanding to know what she was talking about. Mary smiled and he felt the thing holding him loosen again.

"That's a yes," Mary told him, moving to sit in front of him and blocking his vision of the double woman. "To be clear, she only brings the white suit out when she thinks she needs to be professional. Today, she hasn't even bothered to throw in the contacts so she doesn't look like a demon."

Emma lightly smacked Mary in the shoulder, drawing her attention. She made a series of gestures.

"Distinctive does not mean professional," Mary said. " Luke must have seen you in it once and decided 'Professional Emma' is the evilest thing that he's ever seen, since that's what we *all* saw when—"

Emma made a sharp gesture to stop Mary, followed by another one indicating Max.

"Fine," Mary sighed. Her eyes went back to Max's. "Okay, so I am going to get you to do something. Close your eyes and look inside your head."

Max stared at her and tried to move out of the nothing that held him in place. Though it didn't feel as tight anymore, he couldn't move a muscle under it. He was trapped here, at the mercy of this girl who said she was Mary, though there was no way to tell if she was lying to him. The woman in white who had caused his injury was still in the room and looked like she was going to make him hurt even worse. For all he knew, Mary was the one making him see double. Closing his eyes was probably just another way to keep him off guard.

Why the hell am I going to fall for that?

"You're falling for it because I'm going to let you go after you're done."

Max blinked, unable to react in any other way at Mary. She rolled her eyes. "If you think that loudly, of course I can hear it. You can do it too. Now close the eyes."

Max hesitated a moment longer, the woman in white behind her shuffling against the wall, both out of impatience and discomfort. Either way, he hoped she would stay there for just a little longer as he finally let his eyes drift shut.

"Okay, so if you look around your brain in there, you're going to notice some things that don't really seem like they should be there. They're going to try and make you not think too hard about them, but you need to push them out."

Can't you do that? a female voice asked.

"Shut up, Emma. You're going to do it all on your own so you know it's not me in your head. Deep breaths. Concentrate."

Max tried to ignore both of them and just do what she said. If they tried to cut off his arm while he wasn't looking, it might grow back. He'd healed his leg, after all. Maybe he could just tape his arm back onto the stump and it would heal all on its own.

He wondered if this was how it started with Luke and Willow. If they started out kidnapped with eyes closed, just waiting for something to happen. He could almost feel the pain waiting for him. The fire, his lungs filling with water, the...

He paused at that. He could remember these things happening despite the fact that he knew they never did. It was only the memory of something that happened, of something Luke had somehow managed to pass onto him as an impression. It felt natural there, but it was just a little off.

Max tried to push it aside, finding it remarkably easy to make it go away. He looked for other things like it and found several hiding amidst the mess of thoughts clouding his mind. He hunted each of them down one by one, forcing them out as soon as he caught them. With each one gone, he felt his head clear from a haze he didn't realize was there.

When he finally felt like he'd finished, he opened his eyes and saw the woman in white no longer in white. She stood there with black hair and a corset that matched, her red eyes now looking at two other boys standing with her, both of them looking very familiar.

Mary leaned over, her eyes locking with his again. "I'm going to let you go now," she said. "And I'll introduce you to the people who have been trying and failing to help you. Because they suck at this." She said the last part loud enough to draw their attention and offered Max a hand up.

He looked at the door. He could run, but he was sure they would catch him if he tried. He also didn't know what was outside of these doors besides the hallway. He would wait until he knew how to get out of here. He could play along at least until then, he hoped.

"No one's cutting my arms off, right?" he asked.

"Nope," Mary told him.

Max let her haul him to his feet. At his first uneasy step, she ducked under his arm and helped him walk towards the other three, now all paying attention to him. The woman and the guy on her right with white hair and dressed in black. The third, dressed in a green shirt and a beanie, was shaking his head. They all looked paler than Max.

"Okay," Mary said, "which one of these guys broke your leg?"

The girl rose her hand. Looking at her now, she looked no older than Willow. *Sorry,* she signed, her fist rubbing small circles on her chest. She handed him a towel, a gentle smile on her face. When Max didn't move to take it, Mary took it and passed it to him.

Max's attention drifted next to her to the guy dressed in black. "I know you," he said, the memory coming back to him in a rush. Papers all over the ground. A goth guy with red eyes trying to help pick them up. "You were at my school."

"Can we catch up outside of the psych ward?" Mary asked.

We'll get caught, the guy in normal clothes said.

Mary rolled her eyes and brought Max over to sit on the bed. "We need to get you a shirt... what did you say your name was?"

"Max."

"Max," Mary repeated, sitting next to him. The other three took a seat on the floor in front of him in a ring. "Green shirt is Adam, goth boy is Gavin and you've now seen Emma outside of the white."

"What's going on?" Max asked. He tried not to look, but he couldn't help letting his eyes slip past Mary to the door. She was in his way. Her and whoever else was in this building, all of whom might not be as nice as Mary about his presence there and who might want to keep him tied down somewhere.

You're freaking out, Adam said, mischievous grin on his face as his hands moved. *That's perfectly normal.*

Not helping, Emma told him. She turned back to Max, looking a bit more sympathetic and pleading. *But could you not do that? It kind of stings after a while.*

"Do what?"

"Let your mind wander," Mary told him. "It creates a buzzing when we do it. Although, I swear you're worse than I am."

He is, Adam said. *By a lot. Makes him dead easy to track down, at least.*

And screw with our heads, Gavin said.

"So are you or aren't you going to cut off my arms and torture me?" Max snapped.

CHAPTER SEVENTEEN

A VERY LONG moment of silence hung in the air. Max shrunk away at the attention, wrapping himself in the towel and still finding himself too exposed. They didn't feel dangerous right now, but he could still remember what they had already done to him and he knew what this place was supposed to do.

We're not with the facility, Emma told him as if that was supposed to make sense. *We aren't being sent out to try and round you up and put you through all the stuff we went through. The facility doesn't even exist anymore. Luke and Willow are... well, not exactly lying to you.*

They're a little messed up in the head, Gavin said, his hands moving sharply through the air. *They believe it and all, but you're all being mislead. We're just trying to set things straight and giving you an option.*

"And you thought breaking my leg and setting Harrison on fire was going to do that?" Max asked.

"You set him on *fire*?" Mary demanded, looking at all of them, Gavin avoided her eyes.

Being around Luke screws with just about everyone, Adam said. *And he was in your head, so you were broadcasting on his behalf along with the rest of your buzzing. You... don't understand any of this, do you?*

Max shook his head and rubbed at his hair with the towel. It was getting a bit cold in here without a shirt, but he felt calm. He had the feeling that they didn't want to hurt him, though he knew even that might be a trick.

You said something about cutting off your arms, so I'm guessing you've heard of the facility where we were kept. What do you already know about it?

Max thought back, trying to put all of the pieces of information he had into place. "It's in... some place I've never heard of. Hope? Which is somewhere past Seattle, I think. There were people in there who went around trying to find kids with powers and bring them in there and they did experiments and tortured them to make them develop even more powers."

Max flinched, an onslaught of memories coming to the surface from the other three, much like Luke's. The fire, the drowning and so much pain flooded his mind that he couldn't keep it all out. "Yeah, like that."

"They can't keep those ones down," Mary told him. She waved her hand by her head. "Memories."

We'll start there, Emma said, looking apologetic as her hands moved. *None of us really remember arriving there. We were scared and confused and we could do these things that we didn't understand. They called us Psychics and said they were going to bring out our potential. And then they turned out to be horrible people. We learned; and the more of us there were, the stronger we grew.*

We were brought there and they did whatever they could to try and activate as many of our abilities as they could. They had our arms and legs removed so that they could force us to learn how to move them with our minds. You develop a lot of them based on your situation at the time, apparently. The electroshock was the worst. We think they kind of liked it, since it meant that we stopped talking. They mostly used it to keep us in line.

"That's why none of them can talk," Mary said. "They lost motor control of their tongues or they accidentally bit them off."

Emma nodded, as did the other two. *They were trying to make us nice and powerful and obedient. They had buyers, international ones, who wanted extra protection and just one of us paid off the entire operation. They were manufacturing us. But we wanted out. There were 34 of us at first, but by the end...* Emma shook her head. *Have you heard of Rue? Does Luke still talk about her?*

Max nodded, taking it all of it in as best he could. He was still getting flashes of what happened, but they were clearly trying to keep their memories quiet.

Rue was like an older sister to all of us. I think that's why they went on her so hard. She would tell us things all the time, like how it was going to be okay and how we weren't meant for this world. That if we were good, then they would let us go home. To our real home. She had this idea in her head that we really didn't belong in the world with humans who would do things like this to us. We belonged on the other side with our own kind.

In his mind he could see Rue again, like Luke's image of her but much more manic, trying desperately to assure the others that everything was going to be all right. All they had to do was be patient and eventually they would be let go and go off to a better place.

"A better place through the gate?" Max asked.

The gate is a waste disposal, Emma told him. *We thought it was this great mystical thing, but it's just an electric waste disposal unit. Disintegrates anything that passes through it. It's where they'd toss the bodies of any of the others that died, but Rue would say that they just went on to paradise. She got us all to believe it. Like, really believe it. We needed hope and that was what we got. Hope that maybe we wouldn't be disintegrated and that was really a portal to another world that we would be sent to when we were done here.*

When we did finally decide to break out, those of us left, we ended up razing the building. None of us was thinking that clearly. We managed to surprise them. They didn't know we were all communicating at all, but Rue gave us the cue and we got the jump on them and ran for it and burned everything in our path. We didn't really think it through and ended up back down by the incinerator with the doctors that were trying to escape. What happened was... not our proudest moment.

Max got flashes of it, a standoff where the feral test subjects went after the scientists, setting them on fire and otherwise tearing them apart as a means to try and get out. They were blocking the way out over the incinerator, the very large hole in the floor rather than the gilded gate that Luke has thought it was.

Mary put a hand on Max's leg and forced his knee still. Max hadn't even realized it was moving.

Rue threw Sarah in first, Emma said. *And then she jumped in afterwards. She was free and then so were we. It was like a weird cloud had lifted, but none of us were ready to do anything different. We were still trying to escape. We needed to get out of there. There was a safety cover over the incinerator that closed, so that wasn't an option anymore, so we ran. We got out and we tried to figure out what to do with ourselves.*

Except that it's hard for mute quadruple amputees to find work, Gavin said, wry smile crossing his lips.

Emma nodded. *We were having some trouble adjusting. People at the shelters were kind of freaked out by us. Very few people we went to actually knew any sign language. Heck, we didn't pick it up for a while. Luke's hands got crushed a little when we were escaping, so they weren't working right anyway, but we tried to learn enough to get by where we could.*

That's when this genius decided to give a pep talk, Gavin said jamming a thumb in Emma's direction. *We were all pretty depressed and Rue wasn't around, so she thought she'd give it a shot. Told us to try and remember Rue and what Rue would have wanted us to do. And that makes Luke focus. Somehow, he got it in all our heads that we had to go back and get back through the gate. Because that's what Rue would have wanted, all of us together in paradise. And at first, we were all for it.*

And then we started fighting about it. As it turned out, Rue's wishes weren't really that clear. We could have just gone back and jumped in the hole, but she also wanted us to go out and find other kids and bring them too. She said once that there was another gate that we might be able to find that wasn't underneath a facility that we'd blown up. We were worried that, even with the facility gone, they might still be looking for us.

Adam started moving his hands next. *I knew something was kind of weird. I popped Emma away to talk, out of range of Luke and we realized he was doing something. Rue used to do it too. It's a psychic thing, we think. You can make people around you believe things if you* believe them bad enough, and Luke believed it like crazy. He wanted to go back and bring other kids along and open the gate with a sacrifice and—

"Wait, sacrifice?" Max asked. "I don't remember anything about a sacrifice."

That was Sarah, Gavin said. *Rue threw her into the gate first.*

He thought that the facility would rebuild itself and then people would come after us, Adam continued. *We had to stay away from them for almost a day before Emma could think for herself again. After that, we started staying away for long periods of time while Luke started to... well he wasn't in charge. Willow did that. He was focusing on that delusion of his. We were moving around a lot and when Luke started saying he was finding other kids like us, we grabbed Gavin and made a run for it. Willow it was too late for, but Gavin still had a chance.*

Gavin grinned. *Appreciated.*

I think they found Mary and Jaime not long after. Since Gavin really wanted to stay close, we kept watching them from a bit of a distance. Adam, apparently, can track down Luke while Luke tracks down the kids.

"And that's when you started tracking us other kids down like you and killing their parents?"

Emma looked amused. She smacked Gavin lightly on the arm.

Gavin vanished for a moment and came back with two folders. He opened up the first one on the bed next to Max so he could get a better look. Inside were several sheets of paper that looked like they had been ripped off of a wall. At Gavin's insistence, Max flipped through them, not at all sure what to make of them. He saw Harrison's picture, as well as Ally's and Ted's, except these weren't wanted posters at all.

"Missing?" he asked, not looking up from them. Everyone looked younger, less haggard and happier in their pictures than he knew them, but it was still obviously them. Florida, California, Georgia. There were numbers to call, rewards offered for information and all of them outlining very similar details about how they disappeared.

"But Harrison said he saw a wanted poster for him," Max insisted. "He's not missing, he's *wanted*. Because you guys shot his parents and now..."

Gavin shook his head and dropped the second folder into Max's lap. *We knew Luke and Willow were coming after others like us. Rue had a thing where she thought all of us should be together in paradise, so they were going to try to round up as many to bring through the gate as possible. The guys we work for now, they don't have the resources to deal with it and it's just easier to hope it fixes itself. And then you came along.*

Max opened the second file to find newspaper clippings with his face on them. There was a statement from Jeremy, who had been on a call with him and was the last person to have talked to him. They found his backpack in the city soon afterwards. Later, an update to the case noted a pill bottle with his prescription and traces of blood found on a playground. A week after that, a family came home from vacation to find a pair of his bloody shoes in their daughter's room.

Max couldn't move. His parents weren't dead. They both looked worried in the small shot on the clippings, though otherwise just like the day he'd left them. It was all a lie. They weren't dead.

"You got a nationwide manhunt after you," Mary told him. "You can go home any time you want. This whole thing can be all over."

Home was waiting for him. He could go back and enjoy the rest of his summer. He could see an actual doctor about his leg and he could forget about getting kidnapped out of his home, nearly being set on fire and suffering through the worst pain in his life. The confusion and lack of sense any of this made would be gone and he could see his family again, hang out with his friends again and go back to a normal life.

While everyone else faced death because he left them behind.

"But just me," he said.

Just you, Emma agreed. *Or you can go back and try to convince everyone else to leave before they get to the incinerator.*

"Can't you go destroy it yourselves?"

It doesn't work anymore, Emma assured him. *We broke as much of it as we could, but that's not going to stop anything. Even if Willow can't get it working again, which she probably can, it's still a hundred foot drop to the bottom with no way out.*

"Then what do you want me to do?"

Get Luke out of their heads, Gavin said. *Get Harrison to get everyone out of there to us and we'll keep them safe here. Luke and Willow won't have anyone but themselves to throw in the hole after that. Mary's done it before.*

"Mary *kind of* did it *once* with Jaime and it only half worked," Mary told them. "Adam was the one that did it with Jack, remember?"

Max hesitated, looking down at the wanted posters next to him and trying to decide. "Can I use a phone?" he asked.

"Come on," Mary said, helping him up and out into the hall. She said nothing as he picked up the receiver on the phone in the hall and dialed the number on the bottom of Harrison's poster.

On the other end, the hotline picked up, with no static on the line.

"Hi," Max said, not listening to the person on the other end. "I might have a missing persons report, but I wanted to see if it was still an open case."

"Okay, do you have a name or a case number?" Max rattled off the number on the piece of paper, the man on the other end typing it up and pulling something up on his computer. "Yes, Harrison Owens is still missing and the case is still open. Do you have any information about his whereabouts?"

Max hung up the phone. He stared at it like it might come to life and chew his throat out. It was true. Not a wanted criminal. A missing person. Kidnapped. The poster wasn't him imagining things, he'd gotten a real person. He stared at it for a little while, trying to process it.

"He's actually missing," Max said, looking at Mary. "Is this even happening?"

"You're about to make a stupid decision," Mary told him. "You can't go back there."

"I don't... maybe. They don't deserve to die."

"I'm going to tell you quick what they aren't going to tell you," Mary said, pulling him in close and her eyes darting around for anyone that might overhear them. "Jack. You might have heard the name. I left with him and they made this deal with us, too. I stayed on this side, went back home, stayed totally safe. Jack decided to be a big damn hero and go back."

Max already got flashes of panic and fear from her as she spoke, her eyes pleading and her words barely above a whisper as they tumbled out.

"He was barely alive when he came back. They beat him within an inch of his life because they were convinced that he was one of those agents now. And that's what's going to happen if you waltz back in there on that leg of yours. You aren't even going to be able to run away."

Mary wasn't lying, but Max couldn't help thinking about everyone else in the house he'd left behind. As much as he wanted to run, he owed them for taking care of him. If he didn't go, they were all going to end up dead at the bottom of a pit. Harrison's lifeless eyes were already staring back at him.

"You're buzzing pretty bad," Mary said. "Come on. Just tell them no and we'll get you back home."

Max let her guide her back into the room as his thoughts came together. "Okay," he said as the door shut behind him. "I'll go back."

Mary looked betrayed and she dropped his arm, backing away and leaving him standing unsteadily on his feet. Max took a deep, steadying breath and continued. "If this is going to work and it's not going to end up like Jack, we're going to need to be smarter about how I go back. One of you is going to have to hit me."

CHAPTER EIGHTEEN

Max woke next in bed, which he assumed meant that it worked. He felt like he had a good grasp on life, if that life was a rather painful one, and he wasn't attached to any hospital equipment. Instead, his arms had been wrapped up and he was tucked in with a shirt on and the shorts he'd been wearing draped over a chair in the corner.

The weight on his bed was Harrison, his soft blond hair catching in the sunlight as he slept. He looked peaceful, his back rising and falling gently with his soft snores. He decided Harrison would be first. He'd clear his mind of whatever Luke was doing to it and maybe that would be enough to make sure he got home safe after all this.

Now that he knew it was there, he could feel Luke's buzzing permeating the air. It had been there at the start too, come to think of it. It was just a light hum at the back of his head. He closed his eyes and imagined a thick wall around his mind to keep the buzzing out. The thicker the wall got, the quieter the buzzing became until he couldn't feel it at all.

With his mind quiet, he let out a soft groan and forced himself up into a sitting position so he could see the damage. "Oh come on," he said, looking at just how much of himself appeared to be broken. He could tell they were, mercifully, mostly surface injuries that wouldn't take more than a few days to repair, but there were a lot of them. Burns, bruising and his wrist was in a splint. He could tell it was dislocated. They certainly made it look convincing.

The dizziness of sitting caught up to him and he lowered himself back down the the pillow.

Harrison stirred and he stared back in surprise to see him even up. "Hey," he said. "We thought you were going to be out for a while again."

"At least nothing is sticking out this time," Max said. "Ally's gotten really good at this."

"How are you feeling?"

Max looked at him flatly, debating whether or not to point out how stupid of a question that was. Harrison threw up his hands in surrender and Max tried to smile back, his head still spinning. He was not ready to go clearing anyone's head of anything yet.

"At least you got away? I was really worried. We all were," Harrison added quickly. "Ted said they just appeared in the living room and grabbed you. Apparently Luke managed to grab you back from them, but no one can get the story out of him."

Max was getting dizzier as the moments passed. Luke's buzzing was everywhere, desperate to try and get in his head again and his own thoughts struggling to hold together. He wasn't strong enough to maintain a wall around his mind just yet, still needing to actively think about keeping all the thoughts out that didn't belong there. He felt nauseous.

"You okay?" Harrison asked. "Max?"

"What?" Max asked, only barely hearing him. "Sorry. I'm just... I'm kind of..."

An explanation wouldn't come to him, his mind feeling like a jumbled puzzle where none of the pieces were even from the same image. He could feel his voice trailing off and knew Harrison was getting worried, but he was getting tired from thinking so much. There were... things that he had to do. And he had to stop something. The pieces floated through his mind and passed through his fingers like dust while the buzzing outside grew louder.

"You should probably sleep," Harrison offered.

"Yeah," Max said absently. He closed his eyes and Harrison left, though sleep did not come. It was a concussion doing this. Why did Adam have to hit in in the head?

Slowly he put his head back together. He got rid of the Luke thoughts from his own, thinking it strange how much he had accepted them before. With the other side of the story, he saw where the problems in the story about the gate lay. The idea that they were somehow not of this world. The mysterious gate that scientists would shove their dead test subject through without reason. The belief in a gate when they had never seen the other side.

His mind went to Harrison. If Adam had been able to break Emma of it after keeping her away for a day, Harrison might be able to do it on his own after going away for a little while. It wouldn't be that unusual for him to be gone for a day and night if he was already usually gone all day. When he came back, Max could explain it to him. Hopefully, for his first attempt to clear someone's mind, Harrison's would be a little easier after being gone a while.

He hoped that a concussion would be enough to convince everyone that he wasn't doing anything suspicious.

Harrison was the one that brought him up dinner a couple hours later. It was a welcome sight and he wanted to talk, Max could tell, but opted to remain silent while the two of them ate.

"I'm getting sick of breakfast in bed," he said, trying to sound upbeat about it. "Actually, lunch and dinner in bed too. You never get to raid the fridge from here."

Harrison laughed. "You look better at least. You could probably come down tomorrow."

"I will, don't worry."

"We're all trying to figure out what happened," he said. "I mean, they came right for you. That's kind of weird. For what? And we actually got you back. I mean, they didn't just *let* you go, obviously," he said quickly. "But Luke found you and was able to get you back without much trouble from what Willow told Ally."

"Are they talking now?" Max asked, genuinely surprised.

"Yeah," Harrison said. "Not much, but Ally apologized. I think it helped."

Max saw Harrison was nearly done with dinner and couldn't hear or feel anyone else around the room for the moment. "Hey, Harrison? Are you doing anything for the next, say, 24 hours?"

Harrison looked at him, trying to figure out what he was trying to ask. "Not really," he said, his words chosen carefully and he was trying to figure out what was coming.

"I need a favour," Max said. If nothing else, he could blame the concussion. "Can you go check out the area for about a day and night and then come back and tell me all about it?"

"What?" Harrison asked, staring at him with utter confusion. "You... want me to go?"

Max almost wanted to take it back. He sounded hurt, but it was the only way he could think of to make this work. "For 24 hours," Max said, his tone softening. "And then come back. I need to ask you about something."

"So ask me now," Harrison said.

"No, you have to be away from here," Max said. "I can tell you everything when you get back, but right now you have to promise me you'll leave the house and the area just for a little while and then you come right back at this time tomorrow."

Harrison looked at him suspiciously. "This isn't a trick, is it?" he asked. "You're not working for them now, trying to send me away so that they can find me when no one is around."

Max should have anticipated that, but it still hurt that Harrison wouldn't trust him. Then again, it was a strange request. "I..." he started, but he wasn't sure what to do. He looked Harrison in the eye and tried to keep his gaze level. "I'll explain everything when you get back, but for now you have to trust me. You need to go away, just for a day. Right now. Please."

Harrison hesitated, looking around. Finally, when Max was afraid that he was going to reject the suggestion entirely, he steeled up and vanished from his bedside. Max breathed a sigh of relief and got started on trying to fix the rest of his injuries. He was going to want to be in better shape when Harrison got back so they could think of some way to get everyone on their side and convince them all to get out of there.

The next morning, he hobbled through the house, feeling much steadier on his leg. He felt significantly better and could swear that his healing was going faster than before. He hated to say it but the more frequently he got beaten to a pulp, the easier it was to fix himself up again. So long as Ted didn't want to start trying bloodbending again, he'd be fine.

Ted was in charge of breakfast this morning and he had opted for pancakes. He seemed a little surprised to see Max down. "Hey, you're not unconscious!" he greeted, passing him a plate from out of the oven.

"Just sore," Max said. He checked the house and Harrison had not slept there last night, giving him a little bit of hope. He just needed to be away for a day, and he wasn't going to have much trouble doing that if they kept treating him like everything was business as usual. "Sorry about the freezing the door thing. I didn't think—"

"It's fine," Ted said, Max now seeing a bandage over his eye and another on his elbow, but looking like he was otherwise perfectly fine. "Who thought they'd get in the house, right? So what happened?"

"What?"

"Well, they got you," he said. "And then you were gone for a few hours. And then Luke brings you back and you look like hell. Again. Seriously, you have a bad habit of getting the shit kicked out of you."

He laughed and Max did too. "I don't know," he said, trying desperately to come up with a story. "We'd show up somewhere,

I'd try to get away, they'd drag me back. It happened a few times. I don't know, I kept trying to get away and then just... pain."

"You gotta be more cooperative, " Ted told him. "Wait until they're asleep before you try to make a break for it."

"The last time I waited until everyone was asleep, people got set on fire," Max pointed out.

Ted laughed again, nodding. "Right. Almost forgot about that. Hey, you think you can do something to help me out?"

"Say no," a voice said behind him.

Max jumped, heart pounding as he turned back to see Jaime standing there with scissors in hand. Her hat was off, her hair almost hitting her shoulders. She looked past him to Ted, laughing behind him. "How are you with scissors?" she asked.

"Why?"

"I need a haircut."

"Really?" Ted crossed his arms and moved next to Max as he looked her over. "I thought it looked good a bit longer. You're starting to look like a chick."

"Fine," Jaime said, turning to Max and handing him the scissors. "You can do it so long as you don't stab yourself somehow. Or me."

"Hey, I didn't beat myself up," Max said, glancing at the door.

Someone much more qualified was on her way. "Why don't you ask Ally?"

"She thinks I'm prettier with long hair too," Jaime said. "You don't give a shit, though, right? I just need someone to get the back."

"I didn't say I *wouldn't* do it," Ally said, walking through the door. "You just don't have to."

Jaime looked at her and Max immediately felt like he was intruding. Ally didn't seem to think she'd done anything wrong, but Jaime radiated with a mix of anger and fear that he couldn't understand under her otherwise calm expression. Just as a twinge of guilt started to break through on Ally's side, Jaime turned back to Max and handed him the scissors.

"Fine," Ally said, reaching over and grabbing the scissors. She let her eyes linger on Max before pointing to a chair. "Sit. Max'll just find some way to get himself hurt."

Max knew it had nothing to do with getting himself hurt coming from Ally. He took a new spot against the counter far away from both of them, keeping his eyes on them as Ally started to comb her fingers through Jaime's hair. She didn't trust him and he could feel it.

Worse, he could see why. Luke's influence had saturated through her so deeply that he didn't know how he was going to even begin to get it out. He only hoped that Harrison's wouldn't be nearly that bad when he got back and made a note that Ally was going to be trouble for him. Maybe he could do her last.

"Ted, can I get a bit of water here?" she asked.

Ted pulled up a stream from the sink, dragging it out of the faucet and spraying it over Jaime's head. "Say when," he said, Max looking through his head next. His was much lighter than Ally's. He hadn't been here as long, so Max assumed that was why, but it would be easier to sway him.

Jaime on the other hand, her head was much more difficult to get a sense of. There were parts soaked in Luke's influence, but other parts looked perfectly clear. It might be easier to get Luke out of her, but he didn't count on it.

"How short do you want it?" Ally asked, pulling out a length between her fingers and taking up the scissors. "Bald?"

"That would be great," Jaime said, sounding perfectly serious. Ally moved her fingers along the length until they were about an inch from Jaime's head and cut whatever hair extended past her fingers. She picked up another chunk of hair and did the same thing again.

Ted stood closer, watching as Ally worked. "It's going to be uneven if you do that," he said. "I still don't get why you want to cut it. It's not like it's even that long."

"It's in the way," Jaime said, though she shrank back into the chair. He could feel the cloud of fear and apprehension coming off of her, though none of it looked like it had anything to do with Luke. There was something much older happening.

Ted didn't notice. "You're pretty either way," he said, shrugging. "You'd still look better with longer hair, I think. More feminine that way. Hell, Ally can probably take you shopping and show you all the girly ropes one day, right?"

Jaime shrank back in the chair as Ted talked, fading out of existence a little more with every word. He caught fragments of something coming off of her, of pain and tears and a very large hand on her shoulder grabbing her so tightly it left bruises behind. As she faded away, so did the images until there was nothing left of her.

Now that he thought about it, he didn't have a missing poster for Jaime.

Ally swatted the now empty area in front of the chair lightly and Jaime snapped back into view, her face carefully kept still and eyes on the ground. The look Ally gave Ted was murderous. "Maybe you two should try to track down Harrison and try to find something for dinner."

"Yeah sure," Ted said, ushering both of them out of the kitchen and shaking his head. "I know when I'm not wanted. I swear, every time I try to say something nice to that girl, she tries to disappear on me."

Max kept his mouth shut, going along with Ted out into the rest of the house and looking around. "Um, so..."

"We aren't looking for Harrison," Ted told him. "He's probably just out wandering. He'll be back on his own time. And you look like shit. You do that healing stuff I taught you so you can actually do something the next time we have guests."

He left Max in the television room and went off into the rest of the house, still annoyed at being sent away. Max turned on the television, commercials trying to sell him a super soaker coming on the screen, and sat down on the couch, amazed at just how clear the quality of the picture was. There was absolutely nothing wrong with any of the technology in this house. He could probably make a call right now and get SWAT in here to get everyone out. Or he could if Luke and Willow couldn't easily take out a SWAT team.

Well, there was one thing wrong. He picked up the remote and attempted to change the channel away from cartoons, but it did not work. He opted to leave the remote on the couch and focus on the task of healing himself.

He wasn't sure how long it was before Jaime came to join him, her hair still looking hacked away at, but much shorter. He didn't make eye contact, not sure what to say or if he should say anything about what he saw in the kitchen. He could feel her looking at him, but he had no idea what she expected him to say.

The couch squeaked beneath him. He looked down to his knee, now bouncing as quickly as the squeaking, and stopped it.

She pulled a couple batteries out of her pocket and put them into the remote. "I don't think Willow trusts you," Jaime said as she flipped rapidly through the channels.

"Because I keep going off and getting beaten up?" Max asked, glad for the break in the atmosphere. "Because the last time totally wasn't my fault."

"Maybe not," she admitted, though she sounded unsure. "No one caught by them has ever come back before, though."

Max was starting to appreciate getting beaten up. "I don't know what to tell you," he said. "I didn't exactly have fun while I was out there. It's not like they took me out to dinner or anything. I was lucky Luke showed up when he did."

Jaime didn't say anything after that, falling silent as she tried to settle on a channel. Max opted to head back to the kitchen and try to help with dinner before Jaime thought to ask anymore questions. Between not wanting her to catch on that he had an alternate plan while he was there and what he saw earlier, he didn't think he could maintain his innocence around her for much longer.

Ted wouldn't let him help, insisting that he fix himself up and not risk bleeding on dinner. At this rate, Max was healing so quickly that he'd be fine by the morning.

"So have they told you about the gate yet?" Ted asked as he worked. Max shook his head, staying very quiet. "Ally found out from Willow that's where we're heading. A whole place designed just for people like us. Probably more people I can try bloodbending on. It's going to be great to compare notes with other people about this whole thing."

Max nodded and kept his mouth shut, his eyes crawling over Ted's skull for a second look. Inside, he could see Luke's influence covering his brain, keeping him from realizing that this was crazy. It was light enough that he thought he might be able to manage it. When Ally joined them, her mind was much the same, though his influence was even more dense. There were dark patches in her head, like something was being very deliberately covered.

"Has anyone seen Harrison?" Ally asked as Ted put a plate in front of her.

Ted shrugged. "Probably out wandering. Not like anyone comes after him, right? He'll be back."

Ally still looked nervous, but at least her mind wasn't on trying to figure out if Max was really a double agent or not. Max almost thought that maybe Adam should have roughed him up a little more. If he were unconscious for a little longer, maybe they would have let him off the hook.

Max ate in relative quiet, trying to get his mind around how quickly they were able to suspect him but not how worried they should be that the agents could come into the house at any time. Both suspicions might be founded, but only one of them had any attention in the house. How willing they were to believe everything and lock onto the concerns that Luke and Willow had was a little unnerving.

He retreated up to his room early after dinner, where it was nice and quiet and, hopefully, the place where Harrison would pop in and not talk to anyone else beforehand. Max hoped that strange cloud of Luke's imagination would be easier to get rid of after this distance.

After an hour in his room, most of his bruising was gone. There was no way he ever healed this quickly before. Even his leg was better now and he no longer hobbled when he walked. His wrist was in working order and he was just unwrapping it when he could feel Harrison coming. He looked up as Harrison appeared.

"I've been doing a lot of thinking," he said, confusion settling on his face for a moment, looking at Max. "Is it just me or does almost nothing happening here make any sense?"

Max let out a sigh of relief, looking at Harrison as if he were the first sane person he'd seen in months. "Go on," he said, looking at his mind and how much of Luke's influence was still there. It was light enough that he could question things.

"We don't even know what's on the other side of this gate we're heading to," he said, keeping his voice low as he sat down on the edge of the bed and leaning in close, his eyes staring at his hands as he tried to make sense of it all. "And why is no one worried that we're going to have the suits show up in the living room again in this house? It just feels safe in here. And they've never even seen the other side of the gate. How does anyone know that there's a paradise on the other side? And besides that..."

"Besides that...?"

"Well, it's not that weird, is it?" he asked. "I mean, if Luke and Willow know what's on the other side of the gate, we should just trust them. They're the ones who've seen it. They should—"

"No!" Max said, seeing Luke's influence taking back over in Harrison's mind, seeping in like water to a sponge. He wasn't sure what he was trying to do, thinking of it kind of like the healing tricks that Ted had taught him. He put his hands on either side of Harrison's face and looked him in his stormy grey eyes, now starting to cloud over again.

Max tried to push those thoughts of Luke's out of his head to keep his mind clear. He could feel them leaving and put his attention on a cluster that clung to his mind. Harrison staring at him in confusion at first, then a slow building clarity. Max didn't let go, the cluster finally breaking apart and Max tried to push every last inkling of it out of Harrison's mind. Once everything that shouldn't be there was out, he went to work creating a wall around his mind to keep Luke from getting back in.

"What are you...?" Harrison asked, staring at him wide eyed and shivering under his fingers. Max couldn't even feel Harrison's hands on his arms, trying to pull away.

"Almost," Max muttered, thickening the walls around his mind just a little more. He pulled away and let go at last, feeling drained and breathing heavily. He hadn't realized quite how close he was to Harrison, and Harrison seemed to be aware of it too. "Sorry," Max said, getting out of bed and going to the other side of the room to catch his breath.

"What... what did you just do?" Harrison cupped his head in his hand, his body trembling.

"Um..." Max hesitated. "I need to tell you what happened when I got abducted. The whole story. I swear it will all make sense when it's done. Oh, but first," he said, reaching into the smallest pocket of the shorts lying on the chair, and pulling out one of several small pieces of paper. This one, he knew, was Harrison's and he handed it to him.

He watched as Harrison took the page and slowly unfolded it, seeing the missing poster for himself. The confusion and mix of emotion that radiated off of him made it hard for Max to keep his head. "I called the number," he told him, keeping his voice gentle as he broke the news. "Your case is still open as a kidnapping."

CHAPTER NINETEEN

THEY TALKED WELL into the night, their voices low so they would not be overheard. Max kept alert for people who might walk in on them and checking to make sure what he did to Harrison would hold. So far, Harrison's mind stayed his own and Max was glad that, even without Luke in his head, Harrison was still the same person.

Better, Harrison believed him. The missing poster did it, but he was too attached to everyone here to let them all get thrown down a hole. They needed some way to get everyone out, but their ideas were slim. Harrison could get everyone out of there one by one, but it would be difficult to do so without getting caught by Luke and Willow. If Luke could track them down before, he might be able to find them again before they got to safety.

"Was all this really necessary, though?" Harrison asked. "I mean, they're on our side and they still kick the crap out of you before letting you go?"

He was tired, but not from the late hour. He didn't realize how draining it would be, but he tried to stay awake. "It kind of was," Max said. "They probably should have done it a little more, honestly. Everyone's been wondering if I was sent by them even with that much. They think I'm some kind of mole or something. And I don't think that's something they would have decided on their own, you know?"

"That doesn't mean they should have—"

"Mary also told me about what happened to Jack when he tried to come back," Max added. "It sounded like the only way to come back at all was to make it look like I was being rescued instead of coming back on my own."

A dark look passed over Harrison's eyes and Max could feel the mood in the room change. Harrison looked away and Max caught a feeling that Harrison was now remembering something that he would have much rather stayed buried. Guilt. Shame. Regret.

"Harrison?" Max asked, leaning closer to him, his voice gentle. "Are you okay?"

"So are we going to have to do this every time?" Harrison asked. He looked up at him, whatever the dark thought plaguing him was pushed out of his mind for now. "Like, you kicked me out of here and then you do... whatever that was."

Max shook his head. "It was just something Adam said. He said that he took Emma away for a while and it cleared her up after about a day. I think it just made it a bit easier. I think I could do it without all that, but it might take me a little more time."

"We might not have that much time," Harrison said. "We're across the border now. How much farther could it be?" He let the question linger in the air for a moment. "Do you think that you could do what you did to me again?"

"I really hope so," he said. "Do you have a plan?"

"Who's the next easiest person, you think, who you could do this to."

Max shrugged. "Ted? Maybe Jaime."

A dark look crossed over Harrison's face. "Ted. Just be ready."

◆━━━━◆━━━━◆

BY THE TIME Max woke up, it was afternoon and he was sleeping on the floor of a different house. Harrison and Jaime were gone and Max was left wondering just what sort of sign he was supposed to be waiting for or how long. He hoped that what he'd done hadn't been undone in the night and Harrison had forgotten about it entirely.

He couldn't quite find the kitchen in this house. There was so little furniture in here or sign of anything at all that he wondered if this place was abandoned. The halls wound around in narrow corridors that he couldn't quite figure out and he somehow ended up in an empty room containing only a chair and a door to the back porch. He let out a frustrated sigh and looked around for another door.

"Lost?" Ted asked, standing at a small sliding door. Max could see the kitchen behind him, though it looked as barren as the rest of the house.

"Yeah," Max said. He opened his mouth to say more, but something caught his attention. "Luke."

Something crashed down on top of him in the form of Luke's elbow and he fell to all fours, hands on his head where the hit connected. His head spun from the impact, but he wasn't alone on the ground long. Ted was laid out a moment later.

"What the hell?" Max demanded, looking back up at Luke. He got back to his feet, but Luke just kept smiling, his hands moving through the air.

Training, Luke said. *You guys need to get a lot better at defending yourselves coming up. You've already shown that you're not all that good at it. We need to be prepared.*

"Prepared for what?"

We're almost at the facility. You all need to be ready for what's coming there. You especially, Max. There's a very particular part we need you to play. Try not to get kidnapped again before that happens.

Luke vanished in front of him.

"One time!" Max called after him. "Because I love having people come by to kidnap me and beat me up."

"Hey, if you're into that kind of thing," Ted said, getting back to his feet with a broad smile. Max noticed a water bottle clipped to his pocket. "I'm sure there's some very nice women in leather that you could convince for the right price."

"You okay?"

Ted shrugged. "I'll be fine, but—"

Max reached over and brushed his finger over Ted's forehead where he got hit. "Sorry," Max said. "It was going to bruise."

Ted looked Max over carefully, stepping back from him and angling himself towards the sliding door to the kitchen. After a long moment he asked, "You still up for bloodbending?"

Max felt like this was some sort of covert interrogation. "Um... I guess?" Max said. "Do you really still want to do that?"

"That's a stupid question. Come on, let's take this outside."

They went out onto the deck and sat on the railings, Ted continuing his efforts to try and move Max's arm. Max moved his arm with whatever pull he could feel as a means to keep his injuries low. If he resisted, he knew Ted's clumsy efforts would cause his veins to rupture, though he did make an effort to remind him that blood needs to move.

"Does this mean you're still going to try teaching me the psychic stuff?" Max asked. He let Ted tug his arm left and right. He was getting better, but Max could still see the marble of bruising forming.

Ted shook his head. "I don't know if it's a good idea to keep teaching you how to brainwash people."

"What?"

"Last thing I taught you was how to put thoughts in people's heads," Ted said. "I'm still waiting to see if you can be trusted with that much. You have been healing a lot faster since you got back, you know."

"So you still think I'm a double agent? One that's letting you screw with my bloodstream."

"Can't be too careful."

"Is that why Ally's not here to tell us that this is stupid?"

Ted shook his head. "Empty house means there's no food in the fridge. She went with Harrison and Jaime to make sure they actually get the right stuff. Those guys always pick up the shit that I can't cook with if you don't tell them exactly what you're looking for."

Ted dropped control of his arm and Max took it back, massaging the feeling back into his fingers and trying to rub away some of the bruising. They were deep enough today that it would probably take a little longer. "Why do I keep letting you try this blood-bending thing?"

"Because you love getting the shit kicked out of you," Ted told him, only half joking. "Seriously, you've been stuck in bed and covered in more bandages in the month you've been here than everyone else combined in their entire time travelling.

"Only a month?" Max asked. Ted shrugged, but Max's attention snapped inside. "I think they're back," he said, hopping off the railing and heading back into the house.

In the kitchen, they dumped several plastic bags of groceries on the counter and Ted immediately started rummaging through them. Max looked over them, wondering if they'd actually paid for groceries this time around when he caught Harrison's eye and small smile. He looked like he hadn't slept.

"Duck!" Max called across the room, all of them shrinking down at the command. Willow appeared on the counter, her foot swinging wide and missing all of them before vanishing again.

Max knew where she was a moment later, her foot connecting with his head and flooring him. She gave him a look that he could read, even if he couldn't read her mind. He wasn't to warn them that she was coming. It was part of their training and he was interfering with her ability to get the drop on them.

Max spent the rest of the day continuing to warn them that Luke and Willow were coming and feeling the consequences of that action. By the time the evening rolled around, he had more than just his arms to worry about healing. Luke and Willow were gone early that evening, so he crawled into an empty room early just to focus on healing.

When the majority of him was back in proper shape, he realized the house was very quiet. It had gotten dark outside, though there were still a couple voices talking in the house. He recognized Ted and Harrison, neither of them sounding particularly happy.

And then they were in front of him. Max stared in confusion, trying to process why Harrison was there with Ted, holding his arms back and knocking him down to his knees. Ted struggled to get free but couldn't, Harrison taller than him and with a much better grip. "Let go of m—"

Max leaped forward and clamped his hand over Ted's mouth to shut him up. At least Ted's supply of water was no longer on him. Max looked back at Harrison for a moment in complete and utter confusion. "*This* was your plan?"

"Hurry," Harrison said, struggling to keep him still. Max could already see bruising on Harrison's arms in a familiar pattern and moved quickly, grabbing Ted and putting his hands on either side of his face, staring him in the eyes and trying to push everything out of his mind as quickly as he could. His mind wasn't that densely covered, but his had soaked much deeper.

It was slower and more intensive this time, but slowly he managed to get all of it out, pushing every piece of it out of there. As the influence was cleaned out, Max worked to block off anywhere in his mind that it might seep back in, building the wall slowly as he worked. It worked for Harrison so far, at least. Piece by piece, he got Ted's mind clean of Luke and thickened his mental wall.

When he was done, Max let out a groan of pain and fell back to the ground. Ted had slumped against Harrison, unconscious from the ordeal. Harrison's arms were covered in bruises and he looked like he might be starting to develop a bruise on his cheek.

Max reached over to wipe it off, but saw his own arms in the light. Ted had managed to cause some bleeding in his attempts to get him off, and he wasn't sure he'd ever seen some of those colours before. His shoulder was sore too, but mostly his arms were numb to the pain.

Harrison put Ted on the ground and helped Max sit down as well. "Are you okay?" he asked. "That looks really bad."

Max let out a breath, feeling drained and trying not to fall asleep just yet. His eyes caught Harrison's arms as they helped him up. Max put his hands on Harrison's arms, remembering what they were like when they weren't covered in bruises and tried undoing the damage Ted had done.

"Max?" Harrison asked again, taking his hands off and holding them between his own.

"What?" he asked, looking back at Harrison. "Oh, yeah. Yeah, I'm fine. You should take Ted and explain things to him." His eyes flickered to the hall. "Don't do it here. I think Jaime heard some-thing. She's coming."

Harrison nodded and picked up Ted over one shoulder, smil-ing a little.

"One down," he said before he vanished.

Max couldn't think of anything else to say in return before sleep took him.

CHAPTER TWENTY

THE FEELING OF something coming woke Max up enough to roll out of bed the next morning. He landed hard on the ground beside the bed as something came crashing down on his pillow and vanished. Once Max assured himself that yes, this was a different house than before, he sat up and looked down at himself.

Ted had done a number on him. On top of feeling exhausted from trying to clear out his head, Max could feel his muscles revolt against him with every movement. It spread down his chest and his legs and he could feel some of it on his back as well.

Long shirt and jeans today. It was far too hot for it, but he would rather suffer the heat than the questions.

He cleared up the injuries on his face, hands and feet before heading to the kitchen. Ally was helping Ted with breakfast, or so he thought. Ally was frantic as she tried to move several things around the counter, Ted occasionally taking something from one of her carefully arranged piles to throw in the bowl or intentionally moving things from one pile to another.

"Don't you take anything seriously?" she snapped. "We could be heading there any day now and we aren't ready. You don't want them to capture us, do you? You know what they'll do to us."

"Yeah, I know," he said, casting a wink at Max with a conspiratorial grin. "They'll do much worse than kill us. So what's the point of all this preparing? It's not like they're going to let us keep any of this if we get caught."

"It's in case we get separated and we have to be on the run until we regroup!" Ally gathered up her supplies in her arms. "Ugh, fine, I'll just do this myself."

Max took a seat at the kitchen table, carefully lowering himself into a chair as he waited for Ally to leave. Ted's head looked like it was still clear for now. He'd have to check on Harrison later to make sure his was still the same. That and see how he was after last night.

"You look like ass," Ted said, leaning against the counter and smiling.

"Yeah no thanks to you," Max said, stifling a yawn. "How are you feeling?"

"Fine," Ted said. "Really, I don't feel any different at all. Harrison has me about fifty percent convinced this isn't you doing something, but I'll admit, it doesn't feel like anything. Well, except that this whole gate thing seems like a shit ton of crazy all of a sudden. Seriously, why are we not questioning any of this?"

"Just don't start..." Max could feel something coming, his eyes trailing to a spot over Ted's right shoulder.

Ted looked back in time to duck a kick from Willow. He was prepared for her follow up and drew the water out of the bottle at his side, and bringing it up, freezing it to ice to block the next hit. He flung it at Willow's head. She ducked it and stepped back into a fighting stance when the block of ice looped back around and struck her hard in the back of the head.

Willow recoiled forward, grabbing the back of her head where it hit her. She looked up with an approving smile. She nodded, signalling the end of the confrontation and waved Max over to check her head.

Max did his best to appear normal as he walked, painfully aware of just how stiffly he was moving. Willow didn't seem to notice, instead looking impatient that he wasn't moving faster. When he made it to her, he found it was only the start of a small lump and pushed it back down into place.

Willow vanished a moment later and Ted looked at Max. "Maybe we shouldn't..."

"No," Max said. "Later."

Ted nodded, getting up to go. "I guess no bloodbending today?"

"You got plenty of practice last night," Max told him. "I couldn't find a spot that wasn't bruised this morning. I'm just lucky you stayed away from my heart."

"It crossed my mind," Ted said, though he smiled when he did. "Seriously, though, you look like ass. Maybe think about sleeping a little more."

"I'm going," Max said, getting back to his feet. Rather than head back up the stairs to the bedroom, he flopped down on the nearest couch.

Max woke to gentle shaking. When he opened his eyes, he was less tired and sore. Harrison's hand was on his shoulder to rouse him. He still looked tired, the dark circles under his eyes getting deeper every time he saw him, and he also wore long sleeves in sweltering heat. "Morning," Max muttered, sitting up. "Something I can help you with?"

Harrison held up his hand, bruised and looking a little burnt. "Luke got the drop on me," he said, a little confused. "You okay? You look kind of terrible."

"You're one to talk," Max said, taking Harrison's hand to get a better look. "You don't look like you've slept in days."

Harrison stayed quiet as Max worked. He couldn't make the bruises go away at the touch, but he could at least set them on the way. "It's because of what I did, right?" Max asked, keeping a firm grip on Harrison's hand so he could leave. He didn't look up, focusing his attention up Harrison's arm and trying to get a sense of how bad the bruising still was. "That's why you aren't sleeping."

"We've just been moving around too much," Harrison said. "It always wakes me up and the heat's not helping."

Max got the flash of a face he'd seen in Mary's head, though he was in a hospital bed when she'd seen him. In Harrison's head, he was dressed in a black suit and on fire and desperately trying to put himself out when Willow grabbed him and disappeared.

"It has to do with Jack, doesn't it?"

Harrison snatched his hand away. "It's nothing."

"Sorry, I didn't mean—"

The television turned on, both of them turning to see a bride and her bridal party going through wedding dresses. It went to commercials soon after, then the channel changed to rednecks fishing with their bare hands, then to another commercial and through several channels until it settled on a rerun of CSI: Miami. Max knew Jaime was behind turning it on, but probably not responsible for how clear the picture and audio was now.

"I'm not interrupting, am I?" Jaime asked. She appeared a moment later on the other end of the couch with her feet up on the coffee table and remote in hand, changing the channels. She looked at Max and gave him a warning look. Her eyes glanced up at Harrison. "What's with you?"

Harrison stared at the television, wide eyed in amazement. He pointed at the screen, looking back and forth between Jaime and Max. He reached out and snatched the remote away from Jaime, pressing the buttons and watching intently as the channels changed.

He looked back at Jaime. "*The whole time*?"

Jaime gave him a confused look as he changed the channel again back to the news. Max's attention went right to it, finding Tara and Jeremy on the screen. A look of panic spread across Jaime's face as she tried to snatch the remote back, but Harrison held it up out of reach.

Tara and Jeremy were in front of Tara's house, both looking more tired than worried. In the background, he saw both of his parents' cars parked in the driveway of his own home and a distinct lack of police tape from what he imagined there would be.

"He was supposed to meet a friend of ours the next day," Tara said. "He wouldn't just not show up. Max isn't like that."

"This is a bit elaborate to get out of talking to her," Jeremy added, the answer sounding so rehearsed that he wondered how often he'd been asked that.

Max's eyes went to the bottom of the screen. They were definitely holding hands. Finally.

"Are they talking about you?" Harrison asked, leaning over

the couch. Jaime made another swipe for the remote and Harrison snatched it back, disappearing and reappearing in another part of the room. A moment later, he did it again.

"We're just hoping they find him and bring him back okay," Tara continued. "With everything happening... we're just hoping they find him."

Jaime vanished beside him and Max lost her, not that he paid her or Harrison much attention, his eyes stuck on the television.

Even knowing that people were still looking for him, it was strange to see it. They pulled out his yearbook photo and went over what information they had so far, down to the neighbourhood where they found his shoes, and Max found himself wondering where his parents were. He'd given up on ever seeing them again and now they seemed so close.

Harrison kept moving around the room, holding the remote high and never staying in one place longer than a couple seconds. Occasionally, Harrison would feel something kick at his feet or brush past his arm, but he moved before anything could properly catch him. Max couldn't figure out where Jaime was until she made some contact with Harrison.

Outside, Ted was getting suspicious of the movement. Max got to his feet and took two steps left, turning to face the window. Behind him, the report continued.

"If you have any information on Max Kani, please call—"

Max grabbed the remote out of Harrison's hands as soon as he appeared, turning off the television. He dropped back down to the couch. "You guys are going to attract too much attention if you keep doing that."

Harrison looked back at him and down at his knee, Max now noticing it was bouncing. He quickly stopped it, though Harrison still looked worried.

"I missed something," Jaime said, appearing in front of Max. She snatched the remote back and crossed her arms.

"And you've been keeping secrets." Max offered her a smile and nodded back to the television. "I can clear that up for you, if you want."

Jaime looked carefully between Max and Harrison, shrinking under Max's gaze. "How long?"

"Max did this thing a couple nights ago," Harrison said.

"Since I ran into Mary," Max told her. "So do you want me to clear that up for you?"

At the name, Jaime stiffened, her eyes darting carefully around the room. She took a breath and handed the remote to Harrison before turning to Max. "Make sure Luke and Willow are gone before you start," she said.

Max nodded. "They aren't here. Come on."

Jamie came closer and didn't move as he put his hands on either side of her face, looking into her mind to see just how thick the layers on it really were. It looked like someone had already been in here to set up a barrier, but it had shattered, keeping only some of it out while letting much more in. At least he had something to work with this time as he pushed out what had leaked in, sealing up the cracks slowly as he went and thickening her walls.

When he pulled away, his breathing was heavy and he felt like falling over. He steadied himself, and managed to stay upright, taking a few deep calming breaths. His head spun as he gripped the edge of the couch cushion, but he'd stay awake this time. It was not as difficult as Ted's, at least.

"You're a little green," Jaime said.

"A little tired," Max admitted, closing his eyes and leaning back against the couch. "I think it's all the healing and the... other stuff. You know. I'm feeling completely wiped. I could sleep for days. You think we could just stay here for a few days?"

He wasn't sure how he knew it, but Harrison was smiling. At least he was happy. "Yeah, I'm sure I could convince Luke and Willow to stay here for a few days while you just sleep everything off. Anything else you need? Couple million dollars, maybe?"

"That would be awesome," Max said. Harrison laughed and took a seat next to him, remote in hand and channel surfing. He let himself lean back against the couch, absently watching whatever came on as his mind drifted.

"Have you already gotten Ted and Ally?" Jaime asked. She eyed the remote, but made no move to grab it.

"Just Ted so far," Harrison said. "I'm not sure about Ally."

"What do you mean you're not sure? She's going to set you on fire if you drag her away. You remember Jack now, right?"

Harrison stiffened next to him. "That's why I don't know—"

"Ally... she won't handle it well, but she will handle it. She'll have to remember the time she set her friend on fire one of these days. And if we drag her out of here without her knowing what's going on, she is going to do to every one of us what she did to him."

"You are adjusting to this way better than you should be."

"Yeah, well Mary needed a guinea pig."

They were going to have to get out of there soon and he was down to just Ally, whose mind was so deeply saturated that he might not be able to do anything about it. If this was how drained he was after Jaime's head, with Jaime already partially done, he was not going to make it for Ally's. They might want to just grab her and go and hope she didn't set them on fire.

Maybe they could get her while she was sleeping?

He survived Ted's attempts to take him down. He wasn't better from it yet by any stretch, but Harrison was recovering quickly. Even knowing about the bloodbending, Max didn't think Ted would put up quite that much of a fight. Between recovering from

Ted's assault on his body and how much he probably needed to mentally recover from all these attempts to clear everyone else's minds, he was going to be useless for a while.

"Max?" he heard dimly, but it seemed far away, too lost in his thoughts. "Max snap out of it."

At least he wouldn't be the one that tipped them off to Luke and Willow if they ever found out what they were doing. He'd be busy trying to sleep it off. What would they even do if they did know? Kill him? They wanted to save them for whatever was coming.

Max couldn't come up with a reason why any of this was even a problem. Emma and Adam and Gavin should be able to lock down that old lab. They'd already burned it down once, so what else was there to do to keep it from being a problem?

Or they could come in and take down Willow and Luke themselves. Was it really that they wanted him to get everyone away before they went for it? Was that really all it was, or were they still too nervous to deal with Luke and Willow? They had known Luke before and they didn't seem too keen on facing him again.

But Adam could save them. He figured out how to get every-thing out of Emma and Gavin, so surely he could be safe against Luke at least. Unless he just wasn't very good at it. Maybe they were worried they'd fall under Luke's influence again once they got too close, which would ultimately lead to them getting thrown into the gate as well. No, not gate. The incinerator. Or was it a pit?

How did anyone even mistake an incinerator for a gateway to another world, anyway? It just didn't really make any—

Smack.

Max's hand came up to his cheek and he sat bolt upright, looking around confused. Jaime was standing there, Harrison grabbing her arm and pulling her away.

"What the hell was that for?" Harrison demanded of Jaime.

"He was buzzing again," Jaime said. "And this time he wasn't snapping out of it."

"That's no reason to—"

Max reached up and grabbed Harrison's arm, not looking at either of them. "Willow," he said.

Harrison let go of Jaime and Jaime vanished.

Willow appeared above Max a moment later, but whatever she was planning for him never happened. She fell out of the air and landed hard on the ground behind the couch. She started to rise but her head slammed back down the the ground. Jaime appeared above her, foot on her throat.

Willow vanished from under her feet.

"She does not like you," Jaime said, returning to the couch.

"How did you do that?" Harrison asked.

"You know they didn't pick me up in Jersey, right? I've been travelling with them since the first time they were in here."

"Here? Like, Canada here? This coast here? That must have been a couple years ago."

Jaime said nothing, grabbing the remote back and switching back to the CSI reruns.

"I'm going to go take a nap," Max said to no one. He got up and made for the door. A nap of a couple days sounded really good right now. He stumbled getting around the couch, but caught the armrest and got himself back to his feet.

"Are you okay?" Harrison asked, hovering over Max's shoulder.

"Just tired," he said. He dropped, but there was someone there to catch him.

CHAPTER TWENTY ONE

MAX DIDN'T BOTHER moving when he felt Willow appear in his room. He was on the floor again and comfortable curled up on the carpet. Even the heat wasn't so bad today, and his body didn't hurt anymore. He wondered just how long he'd been sleeping to have gotten this much better, but decided he didn't care. He didn't feel the same kind of drained he had over the past few waking days and for that alone, he was willing to give himself another hour.

He could feel Willow standing over him for a long moment. She left without attacking him and he cracked an eye open to the room. It was still dark and he could recognize Harrison's snoring. Ted was by the window of the unfurnished room, making no sound as he slept in the moonlight.

It had probably been a day at least since he fell asleep trying to get to bed. As much as he hated how much he was sleeping, he knew he needed the rest. It wouldn't hurt to get a little more.

He woke to Ted frantically shaking him awake. "Max! Max, get up!"

"What?" he asked, snapping awake.

"How do we get in touch with those people who are going to get us out of here?"

"They gave me a phone number to call when we got away," Max said, pointing at his pack. "It's in those shorts from that time."

"Do I look like Harrison?" Ted asked. "I don't remember what you were wearing."

"Max!" Ally called from downstairs. "Ted! I need a hand down here!"

"Get it later," Ted told him quietly, getting him up and leading him downstairs. "We make a break for it today."

"But Ally—"

"We're going to have to improvise with Ally. Maybe you can think of some way to knock her out before you go digging in her head or something."

"What happened? How long was I out?"

"Not long this time, but you missed last night," Ted said. They got into the kitchen and he stopped talking, grinning at Ally and Ted leaving Max's side. "What do you need?"

Ally was at the table with an assembly line of supplies organized in small piles that looked like they were supposed to be identical, but all looked distinctly different from one another. Spread across the table were flashlights, medical supplies and small amounts of food on top of large sheets.

She looked up to Max, ignoring Ted. "Max, give me a hand," she said.

Max came over, trying to figure out what was going on. "What is all this?"

Ally looked confused for a moment, then smiled. "Right, you were sleeping," she said. "Luke and Willow called us all together last night. We're going to the facility today. I'm just getting—"

"Wait," Max said quickly. "We're going to what today?" He caught Ted's eyes and understood the expression on his face. *I told you we needed to go.*

"The facility," she repeated. While she looked away, several items on the sheets vanished "Luke and Willow said we're ready to head out. Come on, Willow said we should pack a little something just in case. If something goes wrong, this should be enough so we can hide in the woods around the place for a little while until they can come get us and bring us to the gate."

She brought Max to the table to explain what she was trying to assemble and complain about how things kept going missing on her, but Max was not paying attention. It was too soon. He needed time to get Ally's head clear before they made a break for it.

Maybe he could just grab her now. The flames might not be so bad. He had cured burns before, and pretty bad ones at that. Not that he wanted to end up like his visions of Jack, but maybe he could try what Ted suggested and knock her out first. He had no idea how to make that happen, but it might work.

Or he could call Adam and get him to come here and do it for him. Where were those three, anyway? Emma, Gavin and Adam had to be following. They should know what was happening in the house. Maybe they could swoop in and get them all out. In fact, why didn't they bother doing that in the first place instead of letting him head back in there and try to convince them on his own?

"Ow!" Max cried out, his hand going to the back of his head. He dropped the flashlight Ally had shoved in his hands and looked around to Jaime who frowned at him. "What the hell was that?"

"You were buzzing again," Jaime said, going back to cutting an apple from one of the piles Ally was trying to assemble.

"Was he?" Ally asked. "I barely even notice it anymore. Why do you do that, anyway?"

"I just..." he said, hesitating and trying to come up with some-thing that didn't involve escaping to the people who Ally thought were after them. "I can't believe we're going already," he said. "It just seems so soon."

Ally smiled. "I thought we were going to be training more," she admitted. "It was kind of fun by the end there, but Luke and Willow think we're ready. And they said they're going to go ahead and try to clear the place out and open the gate before bringing us along. The training was just in case they missed anyone. The packing, I think, is more for until we get settled on the other side of the gate."

"Yeah, the gate," Max said, vaguely remembering that there was something about a sacrifice involved in that part of it. And that he hadn't gotten much of this training and he had a 'special part' to play. He needed to get out of there. "We still need to get these packs done before we go, right? So it might take a while before we have to leave for all that."

"Probably this evening," Ally told him. "We do need to finish preparing. I think Luke and Willow will be heading out pretty soon, though. They have to clear out the whole place before they come for us and that could take a while, right? They might already be gone."

"Who might be gone now?" Ted asked, Harrison in tow.

Harrison looked to Max, who did his best to look calm despite needing desperately to run out of there. He needed to focus. He needed to not buzz.

He needed to get out of there.

"Luke and Willow," Ally said. "I haven't seen them yet today. I haven't seen them since last night, come to think of it."

"Heads up," Max said more loudly than he was expecting and sounding more panicked than he meant to.

Luke was behind Jaime a moment later, stealing a slice of apple and crushing it into mush before eating it. Willow was by Ally, though only for a moment before popping back over to where Luke was to smack him upside the head. It was more playful than serious, though she looked and felt tense. He offered her the remaining apple.

Eat, he insisted. *We need our strength.*

I'm going to throw up already, she said, though her face belied none of it. *Let's just let them know and get out of here. I'll eat when we get through the gate.*

I wonder if we can eat solid food the other side of the gate. Rue would find a way, right?

Willow didn't reply, instead turning to Ally and starting to sign a message that Ally was quick to relay to everyone else. "They're going to head out now. They just wanted to see how we're doing to prepare. Try to get an early dinner today since they should only be a couple hours. Harrison is supposed to go check in a couple hours like we agreed last night to make sure everything is going okay and they don't need us for backup. They're going to head out now and — wait, really?"

"Wait really what?" Ted asked, though Max already knew and was trying to slowly back away.

"They're taking Max with them," she said, looking over to Max.

Max tried to continue to back away, but only hit the table covered in supplies. Luke and Willow were beside him a moment later, Luke smiling comfortingly and Willow not making eye contact. Max looked up, panicked at Harrison, but he couldn't move a muscle and, a moment later, he was surrounded by trees.

CHAPTER TWENTY TWO

MAX LOST HIS footing as soon as his feet hit the forest floor. The sudden change in scenery and his panic were not a good combination as he tried to scramble to his feet and get away. Luke appeared as soon as he got his feet under him, grabbing him by the shoulders and thinking calm thoughts at him.

He stopped trying to run, the realization dawning on him that he couldn't get away. Wherever he went, they would find him. He was like a beacon. He was probably the easiest person for the pair of them to track down. He needed a plan, but his mind was running in too many circles.

Luke's hands were moving and Max tried to focus on those. If he was complacent, maybe he could figure out how to get away.

It's okay. Just stick close and we'll keep you safe. Keep your head down. We'll let you know when it's your turn to play your part.

"You could just leave me here until it's time to play my part," Max offered. At this point, everything was worth a shot.

Luke smiled and guided him along. *Come on*, he said. *We have to get started. We'll let you know what to do when the time comes. We have a bit of a walk to the place. They know when you teleport in, but you can walk right up to it if you know how.*

Max walked between them, trying to wander off without running, but always felt something guiding him back to the path. They thought he was trying to find an easier passage through the forest, which was covered in fallen branches and large rocks hidden in the underbrush, and he did nothing to let them think otherwise.

He needed time to come up with some way to get away. Hopefully Emma was close enough to come take over for him. This wasn't supposed to happen. He was supposed to get out of there with everyone. He was supposed to have more time.

Obviously, what was supposed to happen wasn't what was actually happening.

Max needed to get away from people who could find him no matter where he ran. Who were going to throw him into an incinerator. He was panicking, but his feet kept moving.

They found a small dirt path and moved faster, Luke keeping a hand on him as they went and a feeling of anticipation trying to get into his brain that he rejected. He kept looking for something that might be an escape route. More than once his eye caught something and he started to wander off, only to be brought back in line by Luke.

It's going to be okay, Luke told him again. *You have an important part to play. We won't let anything hurt you. Just remember to stay close, no matter what.*

No more talking, Willow said. *We're here.*

Just ahead was the building they were apparently going to be breaking into. He rubbed his eyes, not sure he was seeing it right, only to find he wasn't. The outer wall they approached had collapsed, scorched black from fire and looking like the moss was starting to settle on it once again. Inside it looked equally destroyed, buildings inside looking like they had missing walls or having suffered structural damage as well as looking like they had been burned down long ago.

Over top of it, he saw what it might have looked like before it was destroyed. The walls were tall and strong, with cameras that might also be guns mounted along the top that kept sweeping back and forth, looking for something moving to catch.

Luke did this. Even with his defences against him, Max couldn't block out what Luke thought was there and he was at the mercy of whatever visions he had. On the other hand, Willow and Luke didn't seem to even notice the burned down version of the building in front of them, both of their eyes going to the cameras.

Max tried to make a run for it, but he couldn't move.

The air around them sparked, emitting two flashes of light on the ground. Willow had her hands out, pointed at the ground, and her arms jerked from the motion. Her hands swept up towards the cameras on the wall. A little flash erupted from each one before it stopped moving.

Keep up, she said quickly and she dashed out. She wasn't even bothering to sign anymore.

Max felt himself pushed forward and he had to run to keep from falling over. Willow jumped over the ruins and wall in one leap. Max was almost certain that wasn't going to work for him, but Luke was behind him and grabbed him by the back of the shirt. He carried Max up unnaturally high over the ruins of the wall and cleared the imagined wall before they set down lightly on the other side.

The courtyard of this area was overrun with wildlife already, growing over fallen chunks of rocks and lumps of fabric that might have once been people. The trees grew as tall as him and animals scattered at the presence of three living humans in their midst. Still, Max could see the eyes around them, staring and watching.

In the hallucination world, those eyes were there too, but they were in the form of men wearing all black as guards armed with guns. A wall of fire erupted around them, Max in the middle while Luke held it up and he watched Willow leave the ring to deal with the guards. One by one they all went down and she was merciless in her tactics, bringing their guns up to shoot one another, beating the crap out of them, setting them on fire and turning the ground against them as it opened up and swallowed a few of them whole. Seeing her in action made him almost glad he was getting thrown into an incinerator. That would be a lot quicker.

The fire wall came down a moment later, once everyone was either on the ground or dead. Willow was panting, pocketing a gun she'd taken off one of the men that looked just a little too real, but she was satisfied. It felt like she'd been waiting for years to do that. Given how unnaturally overgrown this place had become, that might just be true. How long had it been for them since they escaped?

Come on, Willow said, smiling. *More heads to smash in.* She lead the way inside the building, Luke and Max following along.

Max was getting a headache from seeing everything double. The animals and insects scattered when they entered, Willow pointing at the lights mounted on the wall and Max's mind threatening to explode if much more crazy insisted on happening. With every light Willow thought she was extinguishing, it came to life for a few moments as they went down the corridor, mingling with the shafts of sunlight streaming in from the cracks in the ceiling.

He could see both darkness and the dimly lit hallway and could barely keep it all straight.

They went all the way down the hall without encountering another person living, though Max saw several no longer living ones against the walls. He could almost hear a klaxon or an alarm sounding in the distance. That part was probably in Luke's head and they were ready to deal with it. They stopped at the junction between three hallways and took their stand with Max between them, once again Luke lighting a fire around all of them as the guards came.

Luke left the ring this time along with Willow, and Max realized that Luke was no one to trifle with either. He did not hesitate to bring the ceiling down on them, and Willow developed a thirst for more brutal means of disposing of the guards. He couldn't watch them as they worked, but he could still feel every detail as the pair snapped necks, set the guards on fire and crushed them.

The detail of them taking their revenge made his stomach turn. He could almost hear the all too familiar crack of bone and he could definitely see every bit of blood that spilled out from the injuries they inflicted without looking. He couldn't hear the bodies as they dropped to the ground, but the blood that pooled grew larger with each passing murder.

When they finally finished, Willow took Max by the hand and lead him away from the massacre. He did not look back, worried he might actually see the pile of corpses, but the smiles on both of their bloody faces was almost worse as they ran down the crumbling-and-not-crumbling halls.

They stopped running as they rounded the next corner, slowing down to a walk. There were rooms here, blown out and collapsed in on themselves, but he only saw it for a moment before the hallucinations came in stronger than before. The rooms were intact, and he could feel both Luke and Willow's flashbacks to what used to happen in them. The halls filled with muffled screams and memories of pain.

He didn't need to look in order to see the things that they were seeing, the memories they were reliving by just being here. People, all teenagers, in white medical robes were ushered around by men and women in lab coats. The screams sounded distant, muffled or like they were trying to block them out or like they couldn't scream properly. He could feel the electricity in the air and knew that someone was getting a shock for bad behaviour.

The rooms were large inside, each equipped with differing purposes in mind. One had a pool and equipment for their tests. They would throw them in the pool, whether they could swim or not, and released other things into the water with them just to see if they would develop powers of some sort. Angry animals, maybe launching things into the water. An electric wire was just waiting at the edge to be dropped in for a low level shock if they did anything unseemly.

Another was filled with pits that they would be dropped in for days at a time. There was food at the top if they managed to actually get out, either by figuring out how to move the dirt around them or teleporting out. If they seemed to be too complacent in their task, the bottom of the pit would catch fire and threaten to burn them alive until they worked out something. That was how most of them learned to use fire.

That was when they switched to electric. Electric was far too difficult for most of them to master, so it remained their most valuable means of discipline. If any of them did figure out how to use it, then they would simply have to try something else. Those who did learn, knew better than to not react when it was used, because the fallback was a bit sharper.

Another room was completely covered in small spheres, all of which would either burn or electrify or slice at the touch, all of them metal, and they would move around them, threatening to hurt them if they got too close. They needed to learn how to make them move on their own or risk getting hit, cut, scraped, electrocuted or burned by these things that would constantly come for them while they were trapped in the room.

The captives were able to teleport only short distances in the facility. Every inch was crawling with men with tranquilizer guns.

They covered one another from the men and they could only go where they knew. All they knew was the facility and the few horrible rooms that they were ushered to back and forth over and over all day. All of them hoped and prayed that they would not be sent to the final room, the one at the end of the hall. The one where they would not be the same after. The one where they broke you.

There was dread and fear on the other side of that door. No sound escaped it and no one ever left it the same — if they left at all. That was where they would slowly remove your limbs, bit by bit. They would see how you reacted, if you had the ability to maybe grow them back.

Those that did never left.

Those that didn't were fit with prosthetics. Fake arms that would be much more useful. And you would even be permitted to go outside, as if it were some sort of reward. You would learn to use your new limbs as if they were your old ones, slowly and sometimes with great difficulty if you were not good at the things-flying-at-you room.

If you made it through the room at the end of the hall, you were usually too broken to do more than simply obey. Every little piece of your mind would be rebuilt after that. They would teach you to take orders and to do all the things you would need to do. In the end, they would send you off to do your duty, to protect or kill the people your new owner would tell you.

Amidst the memories and impressions that Max was assaulted with, he saw faces that fluctuated between being Luke and Willow and absolutely no one at all. There were faces that he didn't recognize in there, faces that he knew to be Rue, Emma, Gavin and Adam, and there were moments where there was no face at all, just a person undergoing the ordeal of this place, silently screaming and trying desperately to fight before they were brought to the room. He never saw what happened in the room, thankfully. Even Luke and Willow had blocked off that part.

Max shook, remembering some of the pain that he hadn't been present for and hesitant to do anything. He tried to block it out, though he couldn't withstand the onslaught. He managed only a moment, though reality wasn't much better. There were bones in this place. When they razed it, he knew they had not bothered to rescue those trapped inside. They ran for their lives and left everyone, both test subjects and employees, to fend for themselves. Some of them had burned alive in here, others desperately tried to escape, but they were all trapped.

Max didn't know how long they relived the memories, but he could almost pull away from it. He focused on the bones, trying to keep them clear. There had been a tragedy that happened here, both before and after their attempts to leave. The hallucinations were strong and they were stuck inside them, but he didn't have to be.

This place was in ruins. All of this was over. He had spent the last month popping around from house to house across the country like a really weird road trip. He'd met new people who had been on the trip with him. Ally, with a quick temper. Ted who wanted to be a bloodbender despite what a bad idea it was. Jaime, who knew more than she let on. And Harrison, who looked so panicked when he last saw him.

He managed to pull himself out of it enough to move again. Max stumbled back a few steps, tripping over some of the rubble and falling to the ground. The fallen concrete jostled and the sound echoed in the remnants of the wing.

The echo reminded Luke and Willow that they weren't here to remember, but to fight their way through a hostile facility. They moved again almost at once, forgetting about Max entirely.

Max's control over what he saw slipped away as the nature of the delusions changed again. They were back to fighting and tearing people apart with their bare hands, Max looking away but still knowing precisely what they did.

With neither of them paying attention to him, moving into the rooms to fight off the bones of those who once patrolled these halls, Max tried to pick his way through the real hallway while still seeing bits of the fake one. Boulders and bits of fallen wall or roof tripped him up and he was having trouble finding his way around it all, trying not to look back and ignore the screams of faceless men. They had come most of the way down the long corridor, almost at the terrible door, and Max could barely tell what was really there. The walls had moved. There were armed men with guns flooding down the hall toward him that were not real, but looked like they might kill him.

The sounds of gunshots immediately behind him made him duck down and turn away. Willow was armed and opened fire on the men around her, the gun in her hand too real. They were being overwhelmed and she was watching Luke's back in both versions with a gun in hand, opening fire on everything around her.

Max made a run for it. In the confusion, he would figure out how to get out of here and leave them to their own delusions.

He hit the ground before he felt the bullet bite into his lower thigh.

CHAPTER TWENTY THREE

ON THE BRIGHT SIDE, it didn't hurt as much as snapping his bone in half. On the down side, getting shot was definitely a very close second.

His hands clamped down on his leg and he curled down to meet it, not sure what he was supposed to do. Lifeguard first aid courses did not cover gunshots, or his hadn't yet. It felt like something had stabbed into the back of his thigh and would not come out. Pain flooded every synapse in his brain, trying to process that it happened. He felt faint, but was not about to let himself go under. Not yet. He still had to get out of there.

That alone kept him conscious as he grasped the bullet hole in his leg, trying to keep the blood in. He stopped trying to see reality through the delusions and focused everything on his leg and keeping it from getting any worse. He needed to stop the blood flow, but he had no idea how he was going to get the bullet out. He could feel it lodged inside with every movement, undoing the little fixes he made. There would be no healing under the bullet to force it out.

He tried to breathe. It would be all right, he told himself. He managed to survive his bone sticking out of his leg for a week. This was just one bullet lodged in his leg that had hopefully done nothing but tear through a few muscles. That was obviously much better so long as he didn't bleed out and it didn't hit an artery or the bone.

Luke was at his side soon after. When Max looked up, he gave up trying to fight him. He could see the white walls, specks of blood on them with no sign of any of the rubble. He needed to focus on keeping his leg from making him pass out, even if he was stuck in Luke's version of the world for a little while. At the very least, he might live to see someone come to his rescue.

Luke was worried as he knelt over him and gingerly picked him up, putting one arm over his shoulder and getting him to his feet. Every move meant a lance of fire shooting up his body and he breathed heavily through grunts of pain and a wave of nausea.

He could see now what was going on. They had cleared out the section, oddly devoid of any other people like them in the area. The walls were splattered and the ground littered with corpses that Max hoped would now indicate where the rubble was to keep him from tripping. Not tripping was very important.

Willow saw his predicament and managed to rip a strip of

cloth off of one of the guards and tie it around his leg before ush-ering them forward. At this point he couldn't manage the strength for a glare, instead nodding to her and trying to seem appreciative of the gesture that did a grand total of nothing. He knew there was probably nothing there. What he needed was an actual ban-dage. At the next section, he could try to get a couple strips of his shirt and actually bandage it up. If he had the strength to rip through cotton.

Luke and Willow were in a hurry. They'd cleared out one area and were moving onto the next, like a video game. They needed to keep moving so that they wouldn't be caught, but Max was in no shape for it. Every jerk made his leg spasm in pain again and he wanted to just lie down and hope that they could forget all about him.

"You could just leave me here," he offered weakly as they made it to a set of stairs. Stairs were currently the worst thing he could think of, each step sending a jolt up his spine to remind him of the metal trapped inside him. "I'm not going anywhere. I'll just wait for you guys until you're done and you can grab me at the end."

Willow shook her head. *We're taking you. We don't know when more of them will come and we can't afford to have you dying on us.*

"Then maybe you should learn to aim better," he muttered before falling silent. Willow bristled at the remark, but remained silent and continued walking down to the next section. He felt like he was losing more blood than he needed to from all of this moving around. He needed to be put down, to remain still and to not exert himself. He needed to bandage up his leg. He might be able to heal some things quickly, but a bullet wound was apparently not one of those things. How deep had it gotten? He really couldn't tell. There was only pain.

When they finally put him down at the bottom of the stairs, Luke looked concerned, but Willow waved him forward. He could hear them on the other side of the door, screams from the imaginary people sounding like they were far away and the door occasionally rattling when he presumed one of their imaginary victims was trying to escape their slaughter.

He tried to catch his breath, hoping that they wouldn't get through the room too quickly. His chances of getting out of there grew slim, but there was still a chance. Maybe he could push Willow in and Luke would dive in after her. Then he could die slowly beside the incinerator at the end, bleeding out slowly from this bullet wound while he waited for rescue. At this point, that sounded like the best idea he'd ever had.

Hands shaking, he took off his shirt and tore a strip off the bottom with a great deal of difficulty before putting it back on. He was cold, though he wasn't sure if it was from the building or the blood loss. Carefully, he wrapped up his leg, trying to make it as tight as he could, though he was doing so over a pair of jeans that were getting to be more blood than denim. It had to do.

He laid back on the stairs and tried not to move, concentrating on the injury and trying to think healing thoughts at it. Memories of what it was like not to have a bullet lodged in there. Wishing that it would somehow eject itself from his leg. Now that he thought about it, with something wrapped over it the bullet would be stuck in there, even if it did miraculously manage to dislodge itself.

These healing powers were kind of useless. They could only fix minor injuries quickly. Everything else took far too long. How many days was it healing Harrison's arm? Sure, it was a burn that went through several layers and his hand would have never been the same again with normal medicine, but it took too long. If you got super healing powers, they were really supposed to be instant. It wasn't supposed to just cut down on the time.

And since he got them, he got hurt far more than ever before. This was the second leg injury he'd gotten, not to mention boots to the head and that chemical burn that had started it all. It really was honestly pretty lucky that it kicked in with that chemical burn, but the leg injuries were annoying at this point. And then there was bloodbending practice for his arms, of course. Now all he needed was a head injury. Maybe someone could punch him in the gut, too.

He wondered if everyone else had suddenly gotten a spike in injuries since he arrived or if that was normal for them. Harrison had suffered twice as a direct result of him being there, after all. They may not have meant it, but he still ended up with his hand burned and nearly melting once and probably a concussion the second time.

The spasm of pain from his leg let him know they were moving again. He looked up around the room, feeling only slightly better from his break. His stomach lurched when he saw the bodies this time around, finding them to be far less bodies and more meat. They were charred and covered in blood and dismembered. Luke dragged him onward through them and Max was glad Luke was only messing with his eyes. This floor would be far too slippery to walk over otherwise.

And if he could smell them...

He tried looking up as Luke dragged him along, finding the sky and the outdoors that they were brought to once they had their arms removed. They were never really taken outside, it was just another level down where they continued to be retrained and had their minds reassembled. If nothing else, he could see why the pair of them went crazy. He could almost see Rue sitting in the barracks with the others as their minds started to come back together, telling them all these stories that she had come up with in her maddened state and the rest listening with rapt attention, hanging on her every word. At least he was going to die having made sense of Luke.

They dropped him off at the bottom of the next set of stairs and Max tried to relax again. His heart pounded with the realization that they were probably coming to the end. Luke and Willow were more agitated and more excited. They were close. They would probably be at the gate after the next room they cleared. He could hear them killing people on the other side and he wanted them to take forever.

He had a plan, he reminded himself. They would have to bring him close to push him in. He would just try to push them in first. One would follow the other in and then he would be free to wait for backup. If anyone was coming.

Where were Emma and the others right now? They should have been here by now. He wondered if they had shown up, but had gotten caught up in the hallucinations themselves. The delusions were so strong, it was hard to block them all out. They might be as trapped as he was, reliving old memories and no longer able to see what was really there.

He probably wasn't going to make it out of here. Even in top form, he couldn't overpower the two over-powered teenagers and push one of them into the gate. Currently, he was so weak he doubted that he could knock over a kitten. After they were done with him, they'd toss everyone else in after him. At least he might not be the only one at the bottom of the hole, but that was little comfort.

If he could spontaneously develop an ability to get out of there, he would, but teleporting was Harrison's thing. He wished Harrison was here. He might have a better idea of what to do. There would be options besides just trying to keep his leg from getting any worse, unsure if it was worth trying to heal at all.

Maybe if he just let himself die from getting shot in the leg, they would give up.

The only thing he had left was... Willow. He could try to clear Luke's influence out from Willow. If he gave up on his leg and did everything he could to get Luke out of her head, maybe that would be enough. He was dead anyway, and maybe Willow would be able to see reason. And if that didn't work he could still try to throw them in.

No sooner was he comforted by his two ideas for a suicide mission than Luke and Willow were back from another slaughter, looking pleased. They were ready now. They had made it all the way through the building and it was time for them to go see the gate. Luke got Max up and they started walking.

CHAPTER TWENTY FOUR

THE INCINERATOR ROOM was surprising for three reasons.

The first was that it was the nicest incinerator room he'd ever seen. The room looked like it was out of a movie about heaven, covered in white marble leading to a gilded golden gate, abandoned and waiting now with a slight glow for someone to come for it once more. He knew it was all in Luke's head, but he was expecting something a little more grandiose.

Second was the fact that Max could see the reality underneath it. This place was just a room with a giant hole in the floor and chutes that took in garbage from about the facility and placed it into now destroyed bins. Once, someone probably had to sift through them in case any one tried to make their escape or commit suicide via the incinerator.

The last thing was probably the cause of that. Sitting on the edge of the incinerator, Emma stared down into it. She wore both the white suit once more and opted for a more sensible attire of pants and a tank top. She stood when she saw them, not looking too happy.

You could have teleported directly here, you realize, she pointed out, her hands moving, though Max suspected more out of habit. *You didn't need to go through repressed nightmare alley up there.*

The vision of the gate grew stronger like a flare of light and Max dropped to the ground as Luke, the only thing keeping him up, went to meet Emma head on. Willow was there too and he wanted to say something, to warn Emma that they were crazy, but he could only let out a wail of pain as he fell to the ground.

Something caught his head before he landed and he looked up to find Harrison there, as well as several other familiar faces. "Hey," he offered weakly, trying to keep his head together. He was being rescued. They were here to rescue him and there were people who would deal with Willow and Luke. He wasn't going to have to be thrown in as some sacrifice to the incinerator gods to pave the way for more crazy lemmings. He might be saved yet.

"Oh god, what happened?" Harrison asked, looking down at his leg. Max wasn't really sure how much of his blood had soaked his pant leg, but he was fairly certain that it was damn near miraculous that he was still conscious.

"Willow is either a crappy or an amazing shot," he told him, starting to feel a little stronger now that he was lying still again. Ally was at his side, cutting away his pant leg and trying to do something about the bullet wound with the medical kit. "Wait, how are you not craz — AH!" he asked, looking at Ally who tied his leg up a little too tightly.

"After you left, we called them," Harrison told him, putting a hand on Max's forehead and keeping his eyes on him. "It was a little crazy, but one of them did that thing to Ally that you did to the rest of us and they told us that they were going to go get you and deal with them next."

Max thought on this for a moment before he saw the glaring flaw in this plan. "Why are you guys here?"

"Because they've taken over a year of my life from me," Ally said, coldly standing. "Someone's going to burn for that." She turned and left, Max only now realizing that they weren't that far from the battle at all. It was just on the other side of what he thought was a wall. Really, one of the bins that had been over-turned to give them some cover.

Max pulled himself out just far enough to see what was happening on the other side, not daring to let himself be actually be seen. Harrison did as well, and Jaime was seated against the far wall and peering out, her hands moving back and forth as the battle raged on.

Ally was missing when he looked around, but he suspected that Jaime had something to do with that. There was Luke and Willow lashing out wildly, the air crackling and streaks of fire trailed on their punches and kicks. Emma didn't do much to fight back, not that she had much of an opportunity. Between the pair of them, she only had time to dodge.

There were flashes of something else here and there too. Fire erupted at Luke and Willow's feet when they stayed still long enough, something that he attributed to Ally. There were also moments where he could have sworn other people were there, the ground moving and other things flying in Luke and Willow's way, keeping them from landing a hit on Emma or veering the things after Emma away. Metal bits kept flying through the air and crackling instead of landing where they were supposed to land.

He glanced back at Jaime, whose eyes were and had always been on the fight on the other side of the barrier, and he knew that Adam and Gavin were there for backup. Emma, the only visible one, was trying to keep them distracted. What they were doing right now, he had no idea. Luke and Willow were outnumbered. There had to be some way to just take them out quickly and painlessly so this could all be over by now.

The problem was fairly obvious. The room in front of their barrier was a very different one than a moment ago, Luke's delusions now back in full swing. Emma was in the white suit, dodging and swaying and trying to block where she could. The room was in a solid white marble again, the gate there on a pedestal suspended over a pit. It was shifting and changing on the edges, the ceiling never quite the same twice. Sometimes it was the same white marble and sometimes there were stalagmites threatening to fall.

Ted and Harrison looked out on it, unable to believe their eyes, but Max was just glad for the break. He was starting to feel better after having not moved for a few minutes, just watching the battle and waiting for his leg to stop bleeding. The tourniquet Ally put on him helped but left the lower half of his leg numb. He wasn't upset about it in truth. He preferred not being able to feel it right now.

"Harrison," Jaime said sharply. A body appeared on the far side of the cavern and Harrison was gone, at the body's side, then back beside Max with a new unconscious person. The body now lying beside Max was Adam, blood pouring out of his side. Ted was there a moment later, stopping the blood from leaving and he seemed to have learned just enough to bandage the slice up for the moment, looking to Max for approval. Max gave it in the form of a nod and kept watching on the other side.

Namely, he was watching Luke. Willow was all out in the fight, still not tired despite having fought invisible forces up to this point, but Luke was starting to waver. He wasn't getting tired, no more than Willow, but the more he paid attention to the fight, the more that Luke seemed off.

Would you two stop? Emma yelled at them, her hands not moving but Max could hear her anyway. *There is no gate! It's all in your heads! Rue is dead, not in some magical fairy land skipping through the rose bushes and eating candy clouds!*

Shut up! Willow screamed back at her, aiming a kick at her head. It didn't land, Emma catching her leg and throwing her back. Willow didn't fall over, managing to regain her balance quickly and something smacked her in the head. She staggered backwards, but whatever it was had left. Gavin moved on to Luke, catching him off guard.

Luke doubled over as Willow went back to take Emma head on again. From the end of the white marble hallway, there was the sound of people marching in, the ground shaking as the identically uniformed guards poured into the room.

"They're not real," Max said quickly before Ted's already open mouth uttered a sound. "It's all in Luke's head. None of them are real. You have to get Ally out of there."

Jaime dropped her invisibility and Harrison retrieved her, Ted working to calm her down and all of them staring as the madness started. Jaime lost sight of Gavin and he became visible, once more in the suit and clearly going into as much of a panic as Emma and Willow from seeing the guards.

Mingled in with Gavin and Emma trying to remember that these men were not real or coming for them were flashbacks. All the abuse they had suffered at the hands of these men, all the pain and memories of the time when they had already taken their revenge once when they broke out. It was all pouring out of them and their current fight was almost forgotten.

It was tough to keep track of everyone as the madness began. Willow ripped the guards apart and burned them alive. Ted turned away and threw up in disgust at what was happening. Luke clutched his head, still dizzy from what had hit him and stumbled closer to the gate. Some part of Max hoped he might fall in, but he stopped at the edge.

Emma was the easiest to spot as the one white figure in the sea of dark. She had fallen into the memories, the ground beneath them shaking and breaking apart as fire spread out from her in a slow moving sea. None of the imagined men relented and kept advancing on her as she thrashed helplessly against them.

That was when Willow remembered her. One electric shock was all it took to take Emma down.

Willow continued to cut down the lackeys bit by bit, though the crowd did not thin no matter how much blood Willow spilled. The bodies didn't linger long on the ground before more took their spots and not one of them tripped over the fallen bodies of their brethren.

Luke was the one to watch. Doubled over at the edge of the pit beneath the gate, he was shaking, the men piling in starting to flicker along with the rest of the room. They could see the original room in bits and pieces and for only moments at a time. It was breaking. Luke was breaking.

"Get down!" Max snapped at them, pulling Harrison down behind the bin. The others came in with them, Ally having to pull Ted in and Jaime crawling over.

The shockwave that came out of Luke was something that he could feel coming, which was lucky. It rattled their bin, but it stayed in place thanks to Harrison, Ted, Ally and Jaime holding it up. Around them, the hallucinations of the men hit the walls and liquefied into entrails. Their blood slid down the white marble and vanished. The room — the delusion of it — was solid once more and extended everywhere. Even the bin they hid behind conformed to it, becoming a shallow wall.

Max carefully peered up to see what was going on. Luke was upright again, shaking his head and looking a little dizzy as Willow rushed to his side to see if he was all right.

We need to get the portal open, Luke told her insistently. *Before anyone else shows up. Hurry.*

A shiver ran through Max at that. He could see Emma and Gavin, both of them down. Adam was still out beside them. And they were about to get the portal open again. Or start up the incinerator. He was getting confused about which it was now, but he knew that it was only a little while before they realized that their sacrifice was missing.

"They're starting," Max said. "They'll be coming for me. They'll find me here. They're going to throw me in there. And then they'll come for you."

They looked at Max, hesitating. He knew what was going through their minds. They could leave him there, awful though it might be, but eventually they would be found and probably meet the same fate. He was doomed now, but they would come for all of them. They probably thought they were all at the house and if they weren't there when they showed up, who knew what would come next. But if they were caught with him, then they were all dead right now. They knew that Max was like a beacon. They couldn't escape with him without being found.

"Max!" Jaime hissed. "Stop that. Not helping."

"We need to stall," Ally said, looking around the room. "Ted, how's that blood bending of yours?"

"You cannot be serious," Ted said, backing away as if that might dissuade her.

"Jaime, cover us," she said, heading over the wall. Ted hesitated before he did the same, fear in his eyes and a strong desire to get out of here radiating off of him.

Jaime let out a frustrated noise. "Like they can do anything," Jaime muttered before she followed, giving a grave look to Harrison and Max that both understood. Figure this damn thing out before they got themselves killed.

On the other side, Max saw Willow open a panel on the wall and place her hand on it. Electricity poured out of her and a soft ethereal hum filled the room. It sounded like a promise of something majestic waiting for them, drawing them closer. Max knew it was the incinerator coming back to life.

And then the gate was encircled in fire. Willow was thrown back. She looked around wildly, gun back in hand and she shot at empty space, the bullet hitting the wall harmlessly and the sound of the shot echoing. Max was certain that was a different gun from before.

Luke put his hand on her arm and took the gun from her. *I got it,* he told her. *Open the gate. We're going to need to hurry.*

Willow nodded and went back to powering up the gate. The humming around them grew stronger. She let the fire engulf her arm, setting her sleeve on fire and melting away the flesh of her prosthetic.

Luke moved around the room, narrowly dodging something that he couldn't see and smacking at things that weren't there.

"He's coming for me," Max said to Harrison. "You have to get everyone else out of here. You guys might be able to run."

"I'm not going anywhere without you," Harrison said. He squeezed his eyes shut and rubbed at the back of his head before forcing his eyes open and looking into Max's. "Calm down. We just have to think. We're getting you out of here too."

"They're going to find me," Max said. "Wherever I go, they *will* find me. Emma and them can't protect me. The rest of you have to get out of here."

"Jaime said that Luke used to buzz like you're doing, right? No, listen to me. Maybe you can do some of the stuff he does. I mean, you can get rid of him from our brains, right? So if you can do that—"

"I don't think I can do it for Willow," Max told him. "Even if I could somehow get my hands on her without her ripping them off, there's too much. I could barely handle everyone else."

"What about putting something in? Luke did that without even thinking about it, right? Maybe that's easier than pushing something out."

They both turned to hear Ted cry out, now visible and dressed in a black suit with dark shades. Ally was against the wall with her hands on Jaime's midsection. Jaime was bleeding out badly, unconscious and growing pale. Ally looked back at Ted and Luke, tears streaming down her face and anger in her eyes.

"Ally, no!" Max yelled at her, knowing that he wouldn't be able to stop her.

Harrison was gone, then back a moment later with Ally. In the safety of the shallow wall, she looked normal again and Harrison kept moving, collecting Jaime and the rest of the fallen bodies that were actually there. Luke dropped Ted, looking around for whatever made that noise, and Harrison managed to grab Ted away in that instant.

Luke's eyes found Max's and he smiled. *One minute,* his hands said. *Just need to finish up.*

"You guys have to go!" Max said, trying to keep his voice down. "They're coming for me!"

"But—"

"Do it!" Ally snapped frantically at Harrison, her hands slippery with Jaime's blood that she tried desperately to keep from spilling out. "We need to get out of here."

Harrison hesitated, looking back and forth between them.

"You have to go," Max told him firmly. He'd push that into Harrison's head if he had to. He needed to understand. It was the only way that at least some of them might make it out alive. He would try to keep them from coming after them, but they were screwed if Max came with them. Max knew he wasn't making it out of there unless Willow or Luke to pushed one another in. At the very least, the rest of them could get out of there. They would be safe with Mary if they could find her.

Harrison would be safe.

He could see how torn Harrison was, his mouth open in protest, but no words coming to him. He looked back to Jaime, growing paler by the second, and Ally trying desperately to keep herself together. Everyone else was unconscious and needed medical attention. When his eyes returned, Max held firm. They had to go. They had to.

Harrison's mouth closed, jaw tightening and he took a steadying breath as he looked back at everyone else. They needed to go and he knew it. Max breathed a sigh of relief.

He tensed at first when Harrison's lips pressed to his own. His hand slipped behind Max's head, pulling him in close. It took Max a moment to register what was happening. He relaxed, his lips moving in return. His heart beat faster and he couldn't think, feeling joy and desperation. This was the last time they were going to see one another. This was their only chance.

Max was breathing heavy when Harrison pulled away, his eyes opening slowly. He wasn't sure what he hoped for, but Harrison was gone, taking everyone else with him.

CHAPTER TWENTY FIVE

HE TRIED TO catch his breath, head spinning and trying to bring himself back together. He was alone again and now knew there would be no rescue. Even if he saved himself, he was still probably going to die here. He still couldn't even stand on his own, much less push anyone.

There was Harrison's idea, though. Maybe.

The mood shifted in the room around him. Anticipation and joy. He didn't need to look to know that Willow had finished powering up the generator. The hum was light now and he could hear the occasional crackle as the electric incinerator hungered for someone to feed it. Max questioned what Emma meant when she said they destroyed it, because it didn't sound even a little broken.

They were coming for him now. He took a deep breath. He'd have to wing it.

Luke was behind him a moment later, smiling. Max tried to straighten up and felt a renewed pain in his leg. He tried to stay calm as Luke looked down at him, looking far too pleased. Max forced his face to freeze in what he hoped was a neutral expression as he watched Luke pocket the gun in his hand and helped him up.

Luke didn't bother signing. *Willow got it open! We're finally going to get to see Rue again! Come on, it's time for you to play your part and then we'll finally be done!*

"And what's my part?" Max asked, letting Luke lift him by the arm and drape him over his shoulders. He tried to sound calm, like he wasn't scrambling for a plan. He needed to look calm, to remain calm so that Luke wouldn't turn on him. He was already throwing Max in an incinerator. No need to kill himself before that happened.

Every move now that Max was upright again was agony. While he was not quite able to feel his leg anymore, he could still experience a great deal of pain that spread throughout the whole area of the bullet wound up to Ally's tourniquet. It jarred with every movement as Luke dragged him a little too quickly to the gate. Luke didn't even notice the gasps and grunts of pain coming out of Max.

We need someone to go through first, Luke explained. *One of us. Otherwise it won't connect to the right place and we'll all be screwed. Like, it might still go through, but to the wrong place, and we won't be with everyone and who knows what kind of hell hole it will turn into.*

That's what you're here for. You're going to be the one to tell the gate where to go.

"Oh," Max said through clenched teeth. "And here I thought I was going to be a sacrifice to the gate or something."

Luke stopped, looking at Max as if he were a small puppy that he was considering kicking because he asked for food. *You are. It's a very important task.*

"You said I was just telling the gate where to go," he said, hoping to stall just a little longer. He looked over at Willow, who wasn't moving from her spot near the console, still placing more power into it. She seemed out of it, staring up at the gate in awe and trying to take it all in. He'd never quite seen that look of puzzlement on her face before, but he hoped that meant it might be easier to push a thought into her head. Whatever that thought was.

Yeah, Luke said. *You will. I knew it was going to be you right away. You light such a clear path to yourself that the gate will have to show us the right way. It's a great honour and you'll be sacrificing yourself for all of us.*

Luke started moving forward again and Max scrambled for something to stall a little longer. "But — but I can't go through the gate! Not on my own. I can barely even walk! I can't stand, so I can't—"

I can help you, Luke said, clearly sounding like he was glad to be of service and happy to help. *I'm a little jealous, you know. Rue chose someone else when she did it. And Willow needs me to lead the way once we have it opened. We will remember your sacrifice always on the other side. Much like we remember Sarah. She gave her life so Rue could get to the other side. You will do the same.*

He could see the gate, gilded in gold with the center shimmering like the surface of a lake, clear as anything else in the room. It sat perpendicular to the electrified hole in the ground, fully charged and ready to demolish anything that came near it. It didn't matter which one was real anymore.

He looked at Willow as Luke started to bring him closer to the pit. His body went limp and he tried to make himself as cumbersome as possible — anything to slow Luke down — ignoring the pain in his leg and trying wildly to make Willow do something to help him. He kept his mouth shut, but he kept his eyes on her, mentally trying to tell her that she needed to stop Luke. He needed to be stopped. She needed to see that there was something wrong with Luke and she needed to stop him.

Willow flinched at the last thought. Something stirred in her mind. She looked away from the gate towards Luke and Max, her face coated in confusion. Her red eyes squinted at them like they were very far away and in the middle of a dense fog.

Luke was saying something, but Max didn't listen. He might

be getting through to Willow. He needed to give her a reason. His mind reeled from the pain and desperation. Anything would do.

She had to stop Luke. He wasn't what he seemed. He'd tricked them all and he had to be stopped. There was something wrong with him. He wasn't who they thought he was. She had to understand that he was a fake. He wasn't real. Luke wasn't Luke. This Luke, this was someone else entirely. She had to see that he was different, that he was someone else. Something that she hated. Luke was a thing that she hated and she needed to take him out. What did she hate? He was whatever that was.

An agent. Of course. She's been ripping them apart and tearing them limb from limb. That's what Luke was, really. He was only disguised. He wasn't what he looked like, he was really just an agent pretending to be Luke and he was going to ruin everything. He was the one who brought all the agents in. She had to understand. She had to believe him. The agents, all of them that had come in, even the woman in white came because of him. This place had been empty except for them. The kids were moved out. It was because they knew that they were coming and Luke was the one that told them because he was really an agent.

Luke's grip on Max loosened, sending a jolt of pain up his leg. He came out of it, realizing that he was now only steps away from where Luke would throw him in, but returned his attention to Willow. He was so close to convincing her that he couldn't let go now.

Willow? Luke sounded confused as he turned to her, letting Max slip further off his shoulders. *What's with you? Are you okay?*

Luke? She sounded genuinely confused, looking at him through clouded eyes.

Of course, he told her, sounding just as confused as she was. *Willow, go back to your spot. You need to keep the gate open so that we can go see Rue again.*

Willow hesitated, looking at Luke and trying to decide what it was she was seeing there. She drew closer, growing more concerned and trying desperately to look at him more clearly. No matter how she squinted and turned to look at him, moving from side to side to get a different angle in hopes of seeing him better, she remained confused. *You look kind of like Luke,* she said. *But you also look like... one of them...*

Luke backed away, letting Max slip out of his arm and dropping him hard on the floor. That broke his concentration, landing hard on his leg and letting out a cry of pain as he fell on the ground.

Willow's head bowed when this happened and she put a hand through her hair, looking back up at Luke still confused. Luke looked back and forth between the two of them.

Max writhed in pain at his leg but tried to keep his mind on Willow.

You, Luke said, turning back to Max.

Max looked up and his attention snapped completely to the gun pointed at his head. All thoughts of trying to convince Willow of anything were gone, his eyes flickering between the barrel and Luke on the other end of it. In that moment, he realized just how little he'd accepted death.

You pretended to be one of us, Luke said. *You were going to make sure the gate opened to the wrong place. You didn't want us to be reunited with Rue. You failed.*

Max couldn't think of anything beyond a mental string of pleading for someone to save him from this crazy man with a gun pointed at his head. Someone needed to come, anyone. He didn't want to die. He was going to die and he didn't want to die. Someone needed to save him because he couldn't move.

Harrison could save him.

The gun fired and Max fell back to the ground. There was only pain. He didn't even know where he had been shot, only that it meant any chance of surviving was now gone. His lungs felt heavy and blood welled up in the back of his throat. This was the end.

He watched the scene before him play out and wasn't sure if it was real or not. He didn't care. His healing was just keeping him alive for a little longer and this was life's final show. He wouldn't have television in the afterlife, so he might as well take it while he could.

Luke flew back through the gate, the gate fading away as his body passed through it along with the white marble and the rest of the delusions. He kept falling as reality returned and he went down the pit in the ground.

Willow screamed, the first sound he had ever heard her make, and dropped to the ground. Luke's scream in the incinerator died away, replaced instead by the smell of roasting meat and electricity in the air. He was going to die, but at least Luke wouldn't be coming after anyone. His death wasn't for nothing.

It was so painful and he was so tired. Knowing now that they were all safe, Max closed his eyes and his mind lingered back to Harrison's lips pressed against his. At least he'd been able to do that before he died. At least he was safe now.

The pain stopped and then world did the same.

CHAPTER TWENTY SIX

THE AFTERLIFE WAS very bright. Max let out a soft groan, his throat parched and he closed his eyes against it, turning away. He hadn't expected the afterlife to be quite so bright and almost painful to look at. Or painful in the rest of his body. He thought that maybe his injuries would disappear once he got there.

At least they weren't as bad as they were when he was dying. His leg, at least, felt a lot better, but it was definitely still in quite a bit of pain. There was a second source of pain just under his collarbone that extended into his chest somewhere. He felt it as he let his head droop to one side, so he lifted it back onto what he realized was a pillow and he started to wonder if maybe he wasn't dead at all.

The beeping came to him slowly. It echoed around him, drawing closer and closer until he thought it might be right next to him. The beeps were irregular but steady and sounded like he should know what it was.

He tried opening his eyes again, slowly to let himself get used to the light. There was someone else in the room with him. A few. A few were sleeping, but one leaning against his bed with their back turned. He blinked and opened his eyes a little further. The blurry figure turned around with a board in hand.

A hospital room. That's where he was. He was in the hospital.

The woman at the end of the bed with a clipboard in hand looked up at Max. She looked surprised at first, then smiled pleasantly. She was wearing a white coat and a stethoscope. She was a doctor. So he wasn't dead?

"Awake?" the doctor asked. "We were a bit worried there, but your friends seemed sure you'd pull through. My name is Doctor Lee. You were shot."

Max tried to nod, but it hurt to do so, or to move at all. "Twice," he said, his voice hoarse as he tried to remember what had happened.

"Try not to move," she said, though made no move to restrain him. "And we pulled three of them out of you. You're lucky. Anyone else would have died. Are you thirsty?"

She was already getting him some water when he noticed the monitoring equipment responsible for only one of the two beeps.

Things that were stuck to him. An IV drip in his hand that started to itch as soon as he saw it. When she brought him the cup of water, she held the straw up so that he could drink without moving. She looked more relieved than worried.

"How are you feeling?"

"Sore," he croaked between drinks. He was a lot more thirsty than he thought.

"Any major areas of pain?"

"Where I was shot."

"Good," she said, smiling. "And in good humour as well. Let me know as soon as anything else starts hurting. I'm going to run a few tests, just to make sure you haven't lost anything while you were out, okay?"

"Are those my parents?" he asked, his eyes drifting to the people sitting in the corner. His mother and father slept leaning on one another with a blanket draped over them.

"I'll explain everything you want after we run the tests," she told him. Gingerly, she had him tell her if he could feel that or move this. Max found his leg had actually been placed in a cast and he'd been shot both through a lung and in the shoulder. He wasn't going to be moving for a little while.

"Okay, looks good," Doctor Lee told him as she finished up making sure that he wasn't going to be losing the use of any limbs. "Now, you don't seem like you're going back to sleep just yet, are you? You are going to be getting a full debriefing once I tell them you're awake and strong enough for it. Until then, you aren't to tell anyone about anything that's happened. It's considered classified."

"Classified?" Max repeated, confused.

"Classified," she said. "I trust you know what that means? Your parents have already been made aware of this and are permitted under very specific guidelines. They know they aren't to ask you anything about what happened and if they do, they will be escorted from the premises. I know you'll have questions, but they are going to have to wait for just a little longer."

"So I can't say anything."

"Not a thing from the time you left your house to now," Doctor Lee told him, looking at her watch. "Your parents will join you shortly and will be permitted a brief visitation, but as your doctor I'm not going to let it go too long."

Max just nodded as much as he could, not really sure what was going on at all. He was alive, but that was about the only thing that he had understood. What happened was classified? He almost expected that all of this had been a strange fever dream. He really had been kidnapped, right? Spent weeks in bed recovering from an injured leg? Faced off against Luke and Willow and been shot three times? What was going on?

"I'd also appreciate it if you didn't do that," Doctor Lee said absently, making a few notes on his chart.

"What?" he asked. She looked at him, saying nothing and waiting for him to figure it out. "Oh," he said. "Sorry."

She looked back at the chart and made a few notes. After placing it back on the end of his bed, she turned back to his parents and gently shook his mom and dad awake. "He's up," she told them gently. "You know where the call button is. You'll have a few minutes."

Doctor Lee went to the other side of the room separated by a sheet. Max wondered if that was where the other beeping was coming from.

"Max!" his mother said, going to his side and grabbing him by the hand. His father was there behind her, both looking relieved. "We were so worried."

"Sorry," Max said. He had to remind himself that he couldn't say anything. The room started to spin.

"Don't be, kiddo," his dad told him. "We've all been worried."

Their reunion was an awkward blur. His mother cried and they were both happy to see him alive. He hadn't realized how much he'd missed them before now. The last time he'd seen them they were dead in their own doorway. Seeing them alive was more than he could ask for. He tried to assure them that he would be fine, but they were more worried than that and carefully stepped around talking too much about anything.

"So, where are we?" Max finally asked, the fatigue creeping over him and starting to take hold.

"A hospital in Vancouver," his dad told him. "When they called us, we couldn't believe it. And then they told us they needed our permission to operate and we came right away. We weren't sure you were going to make it."

Max didn't mention that he wasn't all that sure he was going to make it either.

Doctor Lee came out from behind the curtain after a few minutes and ushered his parents out so he could sleep. Apparently being shot three times was more tiring than he thought. He was short of breath from only a few minutes and Doctor Lee affixed an oxygen mask to his face as he drifted off.

When next he woke, his parents were gone, but Doctor Lee was still there. He got the feeling he and whoever was on the other side of that sheet were under very close observation, and Doctor Lee was the one in charge of making sure neither of them died. Still, she seemed oddly relaxed, checking his fluids and everything else to make sure he was all right and ensuring that everything was in order.

"How long?" Max asked as she looked like she was finishing.

He pulled the oxygen mask down off his face so he could speak more clearly. "I mean, how long was I out? What happened?"

"They brought you in about a week and a half ago," Doctor Lee said. "Three gunshots and a lot of blood loss. More than I think any of us had ever seen. We called your parents for consent, got them to email the form over. We got all three of them out and you've been asleep since last night. It is now two in the afternoon."

"Who brought me in?" he asked, questions coming a little more easily now. "Were there any other people that came in with me? Are they okay? Are — Ugh."

He stopped, having leaned a little too far forward and his chest contracted in pain. He was also running short on breath and Doctor Lee gently put the oxygen mask back over his face. He breathed deep and started to calm down again.

"You were brought in with a lot of other people," she told him. "Adam, Allison and Harrison were fine. They're being kept here for a little while until we get a few things sorted out. They've been worried about you. Emma, Gavin and Ted were treated for their injuries and appear to be well on their way to recovering."

"And Jaime?" Max asked, realizing that she was missing from the list.

Doctor Lee's eyes drifted over to the curtain. "She's... stable," she said carefully. "She's still alive, but she lost a lot of blood and the bullet passed through a bit more than we thought. At this point, we're hoping for a transplant to save her and just doing what we can to keep her breathing."

There was something she was keeping in, Max could tell, but she wasn't saying it. Not that it was hard for him to figure out. "Unless I get better," he said, bringing the mask off his face again. "You know what we are and they told you that I might be able to help her, right?"

"Guilty," Doctor Lee said without hesitation or the slightest look of guilt. "Your progress already has been remarkable, and I've been told you can help other people as well. You won't be getting up and doing anything in your condition, but just being near you seems to be helping immensely."

He took a few breaths of the oxygen mask to calm down and make the tightness in his chest loosen a little, before speaking again. "So you know what we are." It wasn't a question.

"Guilty," Doctor Lee said again, now taking a seat at his bedside to keep him from speaking too loudly. "I've been working with kids like you for a while now through an organization set up throughout Canada and the United States. Since we first learned about you guys, we've been trying to learn more. The old guard has been very helpful in some of our preliminary research and we owe them a lot, including helping when they rescue some new blood from bleeding out and complications. You're lucky the hospital let us commandeer a whole floor for ourselves, though."

"Are you going to keep us here?"

Doctor Lee shook her head. "You'll be going home when you're well again," she told him. "We don't keep people against their will. We even ask before doing surgery. But this is classified research and you kids are a bit of a complicated scenario. We can't have you going around doing anything unusual and drawing attention to yourselves, so you'll be sent home with someone to keep you in check and cover up any time you slip up. And, of course, we'll be asking you to come in on a regular basis for check ins."

"So everyone's alive?" Max asked. "Can I see them?"

"If you're feeling up to it," she said. "There's usually someone out there. You want me to see if anyone's up to chat? I'm sure you kids have stuff to talk about."

Doctor Lee smiled and made him promise he wasn't going to try to do anything stupid like try to sit up before opening the door to his room and simply leaving for the moment. It didn't take long, maybe only a minute before two faces he wasn't really expecting to be seen together to come into the room. Ally and Emma.

"Hey?" Ally asked, moving tentatively into the room. Her eyes flickered to the curtain, then settled on Max upon seeing he was awake.

"Hi," Max said, hoping that she wasn't going to keep looking worried and scared. She approached very slowly and avoided looking directly at him, but Emma looked cheery behind her. "You guys look a lot better than I do."

Well, you do look awful, Emma signed with a smile.

"I'm feeling awful," he told her. "What happened to you guys?"

"Harrison got us back to that last house," she said. "And then Adam woke up and we told him what was happening and he disappeared and then came back and brought us all here. And then he left again and came back with you and Willow, but he said he couldn't find Luke anywhere."

"Willow?" Max asked, looking back and forth between the two of them. He wasn't sure what he was supposed to do with the idea she had been brought back. Was she still alive? Did she still want to fulfil Luke's and Rue's plan that would kill them all?

Emma looked away, not wanting to meet his eyes and Ally looked like she was trying to think of the best way to put it. "Willow's... been put in a psych ward," she said carefully. "Without Luke, it looks like she kind of completely lost it. She just kind of sits there now and occasionally sets things on fire or electrocutes a fly or something. It's really weird."

"Oh," Max said, not really sure how he was supposed to process that at all. He did remember seeing her drop and then nothing after that once Luke died. There was so much of Luke in her head, but he hadn't considered how much of her was left in there without him.

"So you two hang out now?" Max asked.

"We kind of have to," Ally told him. "She's the one who's going to watch me when I go home. Have they told you about that part?"

"A little."

I just have to make sure she doesn't set anything on fire or let out any classified information, Emma said. *Not a bad job for a mute amputee. It's going to be tricky to find someone for you, though, since Adam's already got Mary.*

"What happened with you in there?" Ally cut in, her eyes still flickering back to the curtain. "Harrison whisked us away and the next time we see you, you've got two more holes in you. What happened?"

Max took a deep breath from the oxygen mask, feeling suddenly a little weak. His mind went back to what happened, playing only flashes for now, and that was already a bit much for him. Willow dropped, the smell of burning flesh, the blood and the bullet and the wail of a scream. How he'd tried so hard to make Willow help him until at last she did. A wave of guilt over having been responsible for Luke's death.

Luke.

"It's okay," Ally assured him quickly, seeing the look on his face. "We can talk about it another time. We were worried about you. You didn't look so good. Your parents seem nice, though."

Max smiled softly from under the mask and lowered it again. "They're pretty okay," he said. "But you guys didn't have to worry. I've bounced back from stuff from this before, right?"

"I think if you do this again, Harrison's going to have a heart attack," Ally said with a grin.

"I'm... I'm getting kinda tired," Max said suddenly, blood rushing to his face. The two of them excused themselves so he could get his rest and Doctor Lee made sure he kept his mask on for now.

Max wondered where Harrison was right now. He hadn't seen him since he'd woken up, but he'd barely seen anyone. There was probably a reason why Harrison wasn't sitting outside and just waiting for him right then. Maybe he'd already gone home, since he didn't look hurt the last time Max saw him.

He needed to focus on healing instead of wondering where everyone was. It wasn't just for himself right now. He needed to get better so he could get up and get Jaime better as well. He couldn't get a feeling of what was wrong with her, even in whatever awful condition she was in, but her heart rate monitor beeped so much more slowly than his that he was sure it wasn't good.

He was off the oxygen a day later and well enough for long conversations a day after that. His parents did their best to just be happy about that and not think about how quickly he was healing from his ordeal. It was clear now that they didn't talk about anything regarding what happened to him less because they were not permitted and more because it made them uncomfortable.

"Jeremy thinks he's famous now, by the way," his dad told him. "While you were missing, he talked to everyone about what happened."

"So he's going to be more annoying," Max said, grinning.

"Hopefully he'll take some of the attention off of you," his mom said. "You're going to draw some attention after all the fuss we caused trying to figure out what happened. And now that we can't talk about it..."

"We'll figure something out," Max told them. He was already trying to think of a way to push the thought into everyone's mind that it wasn't a big deal. It might be tiring, but maybe he could convince whoever was keeping an eye on him to give him a hand with it.

"Have you seen Harrison yet?"

Max shook his head. It didn't hurt as much to move his neck today. "I didn't even know he was still here. Why?"

"Oh. It's just that he's usually around."

Max tried not to think about what she meant by that, although he could feel both his mother and father trying not to say too much. He let his parents change the subject and continue until Ted and Ally came by. They excused themselves and let Max have time with his friends.

"Can your parents stop telling my parents how awesome you are?" Ted hissed once they were alone. His arm was in a sling and he hunched over when he moved, but he was otherwise his normal self. "I seriously cannot handle this."

"I take no responsibility for their actions," Max said. He couldn't laugh yet without pain, but he smiled.

"Ally's parents are fine. They just talk about how she's missed school and how fat she's got — Ow! Injured!"

Ally made no move to apologize for smacking him in the arm and leaned in to look at Max. "How you doing today?"

"Confused," Max said. "If you're fine and your parents are here, why are you still here?"

"We're not quite done yet," Ally said, her eyes still looking firmly at the sheet separating them from Jaime. Doctor Lee was on the other side running her daily checks on her. "How's she doing?"

"The beeping's getting better," Max said. "I could never really get much of a read on her, though."

"She's going to be fine, Al," Ted told her, putting a hand on her shoulder. "She's probably already woken up and just never bothered to tell anyone."

"Funny you should mention that," a voice said from the other side of the sheet. Doctor Lee moved it out of the way and revealed

Jaime lying in the bed, attached to several monitoring devices and her eyes open. "Someone's finally ready to take visitors."

Ally practically leaped to her side from across the room. Ted glanced at Max, offering an apologetic look before heading over to join her. Max couldn't see Jaime any longer, but he was just glad she was doing all right.

"Only for a few minutes," Doctor Lee said.

It took Max a moment to make out anything happening on that side of the room. Ally's voice was so quiet and she sounded muffled as she spoke, but her words were a mix of being thankful and something he expected from the pair of them. "If you worry me like that again, I will roast you alive."

"Should have tried that while I was bleeding," Jaime said, her voice barely above a whisper. "Cauterized it."

Ally's laugh was genuine.

"Everyone okay?" Jaime asked. "Still alive."

"Still alive," Ted told her. "In a bit of pain, but still alive."

"Even the dumbass?"

"Even the dumbass," Max answered from the other side of the room.

Jaime looked over and her eyes met his. She blinked slowly and nodded her thanks. Max smiled back, glad that this whole thing was finally over.

"So you're all going home after this?" Jaime sounded tired.

"*All* of us are," Ally told her.

"I'm not going back there," Jaime muttered as she closed her eyes.

"Don't worry," Ally said softly. "You're coming home with me."

Doctor Lee ushered them both out and replaced the curtain. "Good job, Max," she said as she left the room. "I have a feeling we couldn't have done it without you. I think tomorrow we'll see if you can manage getting out of bed as a reward."

True to her word, Doctor Lee came in with a wheelchair the next day. She helped him into it and took him out of the room, telling him that it would be best to do it now while it was quiet. Everyone else who could move on their own along with the parents had been brought in to a meeting with the organization she worked for to give them a debriefing of the situation and a rundown of what their options were moving forward.

She left him by a window in a visitors area for the floor to go check on Jaime. Max looked out at the hospital grounds. He wondered if he really could go back to his old life now. He had been gone for over a month and in that time developed things he wasn't even allowed to talk about. He nearly died! How was he supposed to go back to normal after all this?

He wished Harrison were here to talk to. He was around, apparently, but he'd yet to come visit. Max wanted to believe that he'd just been asleep every time he came by, but that was unlikely. He was probably just nervous and a little uncertain. Their last encounter was certainly unexpected and Harrison had no idea how he'd react. He was just not ready to face him yet.

Max's brow furrowed, realizing that these were not his ideas. He looked around, finding Harrison leaning back in a chair behind him with his fingers running through his blonde hair. He opened his eyes and saw Max.

Their eyes met for a moment that stretched on forever before Harrison got up. "Sorry," he said and he made his way out.

"Wait!" Max twisted around in his chair, good arm out to try and stop him from leaving. His chest ached from the sudden movement and he dropped to the ground, the chair following him down. It landed on his leg, sending a sharp lance of agony up his spine. He let out a moan of pain as he curled on the ground, letting out a pained breath.

Harrison was at his side a moment later and then both of them were in Max's room, Harrison trying to pick him up off the floor.

"Sorry," he said quickly. "I'm so sorry. I didn't mean — Are you okay?"

Max winced, unable to get to his feet with the cast and letting Harrison pick him up and back on the bed. "That was unpleasant," Max said tightly. He breathed heavily and tried to catch his breath. At least he was almost used to being in pain at this point.

Max cast a glance at Jaime's side of the room. The curtain was up and there was no sign of the doctor.

"I am really sorry," Harrison repeated, awkwardly trying to adjust he cushions and the blankets on the bed.

"It's okay," Max said insistently. "I just wanted to talk to you. You've been avoiding me."

"I—"

"You have," Max said quickly. "What's the deal? Do you just not want anything to do with me now that it's all over? Did something happen?" Max looked at Harrison, who avoided his gaze. Yes, something did happen, he could tell that much. Something he was regretting. "It's about the kiss, right?"

Harrison opened his mouth to explain, then closed it, then opened it again, though no words came out. Max waited, not sure what was coming, only that it was going to be an apology. He felt sorry for it, though Max wasn't entirely sure why.

"I'm sorry," Harrison started. "Look, I thought you were going to die in there and I really didn't think I was ever going to see you again and I've kind of had a thing for you for a while now, but I couldn't tell if you felt the same and I kept trying to igure it out, but it was never the right time to ask, but Jaime said you did and I wasn't sure and I just... I thought you were going to die and you were telling me to leave. I didn't know what else to do. I just — it was kind of a — a spur of the moment thing and I meant it, but I totally understand if you're mad."

Max looked at Harrison whose eyes were firmly on the bed. He was scared, his voice wavering. He had no idea what to expect and he tried to brace himself ready for whatever Max was going to say next.

Max smiled. "I'd like it if you asked before you did that next time," he said after a few moments of silence. Harrison looked back up at him, wide eyed and worried that he had heard wrong. "And maybe take things kinda slow. I haven't really done this before."

Harrison smiled wide enough that it reached his eyes. "How about we catch a movie once you finally get out of here?"

"Yeah," Max said, smiling stupidly back. "It's a date."

ABOUT THE AUTHOR

TANYA LISLE IS a novelist from Metro Vancouver, British Columbia, who has series littered across genres from supernatural horror to young adult fantasy. She began writing in elementary school, when she started turning homework assignments into short stories and continued this trend well into university. While attending Simon Fraser University, she developed an appreciation for public domain crossovers and cross-platform narratives. She has a shelf full of notebooks with more story ideas than pens lost to the depths of her bag. Now she writes incessantly in hopes of finishing all of them.

Thankfully, her cat, Remy, has figured out how to shut off Tanya's computer when she needs to take a break.